BROKEN WINGS

BROKEN REBEL BROTHERHOOD: NEXT GENERATION

ANDI RHODES

Copyright © 2021 by Andi Rhodes

All rights reserved.

No part of this book may be reproduced in any form or by any electronic or mechanical means, including information storage and retrieval systems, without written permission from the author, except for the use of brief quotations in a book review.

Cover Artwork - © Amanda Walker PA & Design Services

Editors - Darcie Fisher at Into the Grey Author Services and Nicole Cypher

For Sandy, Patti, Lisa, Tammie and Wendy - Thank you so much for allowing me the honor of immortalizing Sandy's Lingerie & Gifts, and all of you, in this book. It was a pleasure to meet you and I'm glad I had the opportunity to explore the store before it closed. I can only hope that I did it justice!

ALSO BY ANDI RHODES

Broken Rebel Brotherhood

Broken Souls

Broken Innocence

Broken Boundaries

Broken Rebel Brotherhood: Complete Series Box set

Broken Rebel Brotherhood: Next Generation

Broken Hearts

Broken Wings

Broken Mind

Bastards and Badges

Stark Revenge

Slade's Fall

Jett's Guard

Soulless Kings MC

Fender

Joker

Piston

Greaser

Riker

Trainwreck

Squirrel

Gibson

Satan's Legacy MC

Snow's Angel

Toga's Demons

Magic's Torment

BROKEN REBEL BROTHERHOOD
THE ORIGINALS

I broke my rules for you.
-Unknown

PROLOGUE

LILA

"Don't forget about the Survivor's Celebration today."

I pull my cell phone away from my face and glare at the screen. Like I could forget about Tillie's big event. Like I could forget about anything related to the club or Tillie and her 'incredible accomplishments'. No one will let me forget.

I tap the speakerphone icon. "I won't Dad," I assure him, as I roll my eyes.

Cammi slaps a hand over her mouth to stifle her laugh. She's my best friend, my ride or die, my sidekick for all things trouble.

"It starts in an hour, you know," he reminds me.

"I know." I sigh dramatically. "How could I forget?"

"You better lose the attitude little girl."

"Sorry, Daddy."

Again, I roll my eyes. I've learned how to play the role he wants me to play, the role the entire club wants me to play. I'm the youngest child of the Broken Rebel Brotherhood founding members and I've felt that every single day of my life. I love my family, the club, but I want the chance to live my own life. I need to figure out who I am without the club at my back.

"We'll see you soon."

"I may be late. Cammi and I are studying for finals."

The lie slips off my tongue easier than it should. Then again, I've lied to my parents a lot lately. For example, they think I still live in the dorms on campus when in actuality, I moved out at the end of last semester so I could live with my boyfriend, Drake.

I try to ignore the pain that hits me when I think of Drake. The bitterness. He kicked me out after a few weeks, saying that he 'needed space' and I've since been staying with Cammi and her younger sister and older brother. I know that if they knew the truth, the full force of the Brotherhood would be paying him a visit and that's the last thing I need.

"Just don't be too late. You know how much this means to Tillie and with everything that she's been through lately, I'd hate to see her disappointed."

"I'll do my best," I tell him. "I promise."

You're going straight to Hell for that, Lila Rose.

I may not be bothered by lying to my parents but one thing I pride myself on is never making a promise that I can't keep. Or won't keep. But sometimes the situation warrants a break from the norm. And today is definitely one of those times.

Drake called me yesterday and invited me to a party at his place. He even said I could invite Cammi, who he never got along with. I know that there'll be drugs and that was why he needed that space in the first place, but I convince myself that I can overlook that. That the drugs don't matter. Because I love him.

"Love you," Dad says before disconnecting the call.

"Holy shit, Lila," Cammi exclaims as soon as she sees that

the call has ended. "You know you're not going to make it to that Celebration."

I drop my phone on my lap. "I know. But how can I pass up this party, Cam? Drake has been weird lately and I'm hoping that the fact that he wants me there is a step in the right direction."

"Drake is an asshole." There's a bite to her tone that I'm getting used to any time Drake is brought up.

"Why did you agree to come then?" I snap back. "I can go by myself."

"Well, for one, I'm not going to let you go alone," she replies with less heat behind the words. "And two, it's a fucking party."

We both fall back onto her bed and giggle like high school girls rather than the nineteen-year-olds we are. Neither one of us had what you would call a normal childhood. There was always some danger or another that the Brotherhood was fighting, which meant that I wasn't granted much freedom. As for Cammi, she and her younger sister, Carmen, were raised by their older brother Cooper. Cooper has shielded them both from as much as humanly possible.

A knock on the door startles us both and we quickly pull ourselves together.

"What?" Cammi calls out.

"Can I come in?" her brother asks.

She rolls her eyes, much like I did. "If you have to."

The door swings open and Cooper steps through. Every time I see him it's like a sucker punch to the gut. He's fucking hot as hell. And he's also six years older than me and totally off-limits.

"I thought you two were going to that celebration thing?"

His gaze swings from Cammi to me. Butterflies dance in my belly at his scrutiny, even though his stare doesn't even come close to indicating he's feeling what I'm feeling.

"Oh, we are," I assure him when Cammi remains silent. "We, um, just wanted to get some last-minute studying in for finals."

Cooper folds his arms over his chest and black ink peeks out from under the sleeve of his t-shirt. I've never seen what his tattoo is, but it looks like a bottom rocker of an MC tattoo. Anytime I've brought it up with Cammi, she shuts down, so I quit asking. It's intriguing though.

"Where are your books?" Cooper looks around the room. "Don't you need books to study?"

Shit!

"We just put them away," Cammi rushes to explain. "We need to change and then we'll be good to go."

Cooper sighs and scrubs a hand over his beard. He looks tired but then again, he always looks tired. I know he owns his own tattoo shop so it must be all the hours he's putting in there.

"Okay. Don't be home too late though."

"We won't."

Cammi jumps up and gives her brother a hug. It takes a minute, but he wraps his arms around her to return the gesture. As much shit as she gives her brother, Cammi loves him.

After Cooper closes the door behind him, Cammi whirls around to face me.

"Now the fun begins." A huge grin spreads across her face. "Where do you want to stop to switch outfits? Because if we leave here in anything less than a baggy hoodie and jeans, Cooper will have a fit."

"We can change at Drake's apartment." I lean down to pick up the bag I already packed for just that purpose. "That's why we're going early." I wiggle my eyebrows at her.

"Works for me."

It takes us another half hour to get out of the house

because Cooper grilled Cammi, again, about what we were doing and when we'd be back. Apparently, he was satisfied with the answers because he didn't give her as much shit as he normally would about her driving their shared Honda Civic.

It takes ten minutes to make the drive to Drake's apartment and when we pull into the parking lot, I see him standing outside on his balcony, as if watching for me. I open the passenger door and step out, waving to him when I shut the door behind me.

He waves back and smiles, but the smile slips when he sees Cammi step out on the other side. Drake quickly masks his reaction but it's too late. For a moment, I consider saying 'fuck this' and going to the Survivor Celebration that Tillie throws for the residents of her domestic violence shelter, but the idea quickly disappears.

I want to have fun for real, not spend my Saturday pretending. With my new resolve in place, Cammi and I walk inside. Drake says it's okay if we use the bathroom to get ready and we do just that.

If I had known what would be waiting for me on the other side of all of my fun, I'd have gone with my gut and gotten the fuck out of Dodge.

1

COOPER

"You know she's just going to stop somewhere and change her clothes, right?"

I drop the curtain and turn from my spot at the front window. Carmen is sitting on the couch with her chin in her hands and her elbows resting on the back. The smile on her face slips and I make every effort to form a smile of my own so that she knows I'm not mad.

"Is your homework done?" I ask, rather than respond to her statement.

"It's Saturday Coop," she whines in a way that only teenage girls can do. "I can do it tomorrow."

I run my fingers through my hair and drop my chin. I force myself to take a few deep breaths to regulate my temper. I have a short fuse, just like my old man, but I refuse to let that bomb blow, especially in front of my sisters. Cammi may be nineteen and she's got the attitude to stand up to me, but Carmen is only fourteen and still has time to have a few years of a normal childhood.

"At least get it started." I take a few steps toward the

couch but stop myself when she straightens. "I'll order some pizza for dinner so you can work on it until it gets here."

"Fine." She sighs dramatically and makes her way toward the hallway that leads to her bedroom. "And for the record, you know I'm right about Cammi changing her clothes."

I watch as Carmen walks away and grit my teeth when she slams her door. Music drifts through the house as she cranks up the volume and I fight the urge to make her turn it down. That's something our parents would have done, although for very different reasons.

I stride into the kitchen and snag a beer from the fridge. I flip the cap onto the counter and take a long pull, letting the cool brew glide down my throat. As I stand there, I think about Carmen's words.

Contrary to popular belief, at least the beliefs of my sisters, I'm not an idiot. I know the bag Cammi had slung over her shoulder had different clothes. I also know she's in college and there are some things that I just can't control. Besides, I'm her brother, not her father.

I dig my cell out of my pocket and order pizza for Carmen and me. It'll be here in thirty minutes, according to the pre-pubescent sounding boy that took the order. Plenty of time to start my evening routine of obsessively checking all the windows and doors to make sure they're still locked.

I leave Cammi's room for last. Not because I trust that she actually shut her window after smoking the joint she didn't think I could smell but because I know that Lila's scent will also linger and I'm already on edge. No need to add to it by lusting after my little sister's best friend.

Before I get the chance to check Cammi's room, the doorbell rings. Before I can even turn to go answer it, Carmen's door flies open, and she whizzes past me.

"Pizza's here," she calls as she passes.

I open my mouth to demand that she wait for me to

answer the door, but I slam it shut before any words come out. I remind myself that we're not in Nevada anymore and I did all the right things to make sure we weren't followed to Indiana. No monsters are going to show up at our doorstep.

I absently rub my bicep where there's a permanent reminder of our past. As a tattoo artist, I could cover up the ink easily, but I like the reminder of where we came from. It also helps me remember why I'm a single twenty-five-year-old man with the responsibilities of a forty-year-old father.

"Are you going to stand there all night or are you going to eat?"

I glance at Carmen and notice her cheek bulging with food. I shake my head to dispel the thoughts that are swirling and force my feet to move. Carmen whirls around and makes her way to the kitchen table, where she plops down on a chair and grabs another slice of pizza to add to her plate.

"Did you get any of that homework done?" I ask as I sit across from her.

"Some of it," she says around a mouthful of crust and cheese.

She swipes her mouth with the back of her hand and for a brief moment, I question my parenting skills. Reminding myself that I'm not actually a parent, I grab a slice for myself and take a bite.

"What do you know about this Survivor's Celebration Cammi went to?" I ask.

I know what Cammi and Lila told me but Carmen's statement about the girls changing their clothes is getting to me. I've seen a lot in my twenty-five years, not nearly enough of it good.

"I know that you're an idiot if you think that's where they're really going."

"Lila wouldn't disappoint her family and Cammi knows better than to lie to me."

"Earth to Cooper," Carmen says dramatically as she rolls her eyes. "Cammi lies to you all the time. And Lila thinks she's in love with Drake so she's—"

"Drake?" I demand.

"Lila's boyfriend. Or ex-boyfriend." Carmen shrugs. "I don't know anymore. What I do know is she wants him back. Cammi doesn't like Drake though but she puts up with him to make Lila happy."

"How do you know all of this?"

"I pay attention. Plus, I can hear everything that goes on in Cammi's room through the vents."

For the first time, I'm grateful that my sex life is non-existent because my room is on the other side of Carmen's, and no doubt she'd have a field day if she heard that. As thoughts swirl in my head about Cammi and Lila and whoever the fuck this Drake guy is, I manage to put back two more pieces of pizza.

"I'm done," Carmen announces. "Can I be excused?"

She's got some manners. I've done something right.

"Yeah." I stand from the table and by the time I pick up the half-empty box, Carmen is already racing for her bedroom. "Keep the music down," I shout just before her bedroom door slams.

Once again, music blares through the walls and I roll my eyes at the fact that she didn't listen. Oh well. If loud music makes her happy, who am I to deny her that? If it pisses off the neighbors, I'll deal with it then.

Unable to shake the uneasy feeling I've had since Carmen put crazy ideas in my head about Cammi and Lila, I pull my cell phone out of my pocket and call Cammi. The call goes straight to voicemail and I curse Cammi for not keeping her phone charged. She's glued to that thing, but she never remembers to take a charger with her when she leaves the house.

Next, I call Lila and while it rings, she doesn't answer. Her voicemail is full so I can't do anything but hang up. I shove my phone back into my pocket and flop down on the couch. My legs hang over the end, but I don't care.

After putting in a few hours at my tattoo shop, The Ink Spot, and then dealing with responsibilities and worry, I'm exhausted. Factor in the last week spent interviewing ten prospective artists for the shop and observing them completing a tattoo and I'm done. My brain is fried.

I roll to my side to grab the remote and flip on the TV. There's nothing on but reruns of Dateline so I settle on that but keep the volume down. Maybe I can catch a little sleep before Cammi and Lila return home. Doubtful, but a guy can hope.

I do manage to doze off and when a banging noise wakes me, I'm off the couch in a flash and turning in circles trying to take in my surroundings. The room is dark, and I realize that Carmen must have turned the TV off at some point. I also notice that her music is no longer blaring so she's probably asleep.

The pounding sound breaks the silence and I whirl toward the front door and see a shadow behind the glass. My muscles tense and my heart rate speeds up with each step I take to see who it is.

"Open the fucking door, Coop!"

Cammi's voice penetrates the fog that still lingers in my brain from sleep. I yank the front door open and the ground beneath my feet shifts as I take in Cammi's bloody clothes and Lila's crumpled form at her feet.

"What the hell happened?" I snarl, unable to make my body work to do anything other than stare. "Who did this? Are you hurt? Why didn't you—"

"Cooper," Cammi shouts at the same time her fists hit my

chest. "I'll answer your damn questions, but can you get her inside first?"

I shake my head as if that will make the scene in front of me disappear. When it doesn't, I somehow manage to bend down and lift Lila into my arms. Her weight is so slight, I barely feel it, but the weight of the situation is heavy.

"What's going on?" I lift my gaze from Lila's battered face and see Carmen standing in the hallway, rubbing the sleep from her eyes. "Cooper? What happened?" The fear in Carmen's voice reminds me of everything she's seen in her short life and I hate that this is what she woke up to.

"Go back to bed, Carmen." I force a smile in the hopes that it will ease her mind. "It's safe. I promise." I silently beg the universe to not make a liar out of me.

Carmen, for once, does as she's told, and when her door clicks shut, I quickly stride to Cammi's room and lay Lila on the bed. When I straighten, Cammi is standing next to me and she's crying and visibly shaking.

"You better start talking, Cam."

She nods. "Um, well, don't get mad but we—"

"Don't get mad?" I growl. Lila stirs on the mattress at the sound of my raised voice so I force myself to take several deep breaths so I can speak more calmly. "Tell me what happened? Every single detail."

Cammi heaves a sigh and sits on the bed next to her friend. She lifts her hand and rests it in her lap. "We didn't go to the Survivor's Celebration like we said."

"No shit," I scoff.

"Do you want me to tell you what happened or not?" Cammi snaps. When I give a curt nod, she continues. "Lila's boyfriend invited us to a party at his place. Honestly, Drake's a douchebag but Lila wanted to go." Cammi pauses and looks at me with fire in her eyes. "Turns out, there wasn't a party at all. At least, not the kind we thought there'd be. The asshole invited some of his friends and when we got there, everything seemed fine. Drake said everyone was coming later. Lila and I spent an hour in the bathroom getting changed and redoing our makeup." When I open my mouth to chastise her, she holds her hand up to silence me. "By the time we were done, the music was cranked up and we were both hyped up to have some fun."

Cammi turns her face away from my glare and fixes her gaze on her friend. I follow suit and my heart lurches at the sight of dried blood caking Lila's face and the way her clothes are torn in places that only make my imagination run wild with rage at what else Cammi has to tell me about what happened.

"Finish telling me," I command, leaving no room in my tone for argument.

Cammi takes a deep breath and holds it for so long I fear she'll pass out. When she exhales, it's full of anger and a hint of sadness. "At first, things were fine. We were all sitting around, listening to music, drinking, and laughing. I started to feel way more buzzed than I should have been." Cammi pauses and rubs a hand over her forehead before locking eyes with mine. "Coop, I don't know what happened next." She shakes her head as if trying to dislodge the details. "The next thing I know, I'm waking up on the bathroom floor and there's nothing but silence surrounding me."

"You were drugged?" I begin to pace, my mind once again racing with the possibilities.

"No… yes… hell, I don't know. I guess that makes sense." Cammi rises from her spot on the bed and steps in front of me, forcing me to stand still. "I found Lila in the bedroom, lying in a heap on floor, hands and feet tied with rope." Her anger wanes and her eyes become glassy with tears. "Everyone else was gone. I looked everywhere but it's like no one else was ever there. Lila was barely conscious, but I was able to get her arms and legs free. She insisted I bring her here instead of the hospital." Cammi reaches into her back pocket and pulls out a piece of folded paper. "I wasn't going to listen to her. At least, until I read this."

Cammi hands me the paper and I snatch it from her grasp, my hand shaking as I open it up to read it. The words on the page jump out at me and in an instant, I know that shit is going to hit the fan in ways we've never experienced before. The crinkle of the paper in my fist reaches my ears but it's as if I'm under water. My head spins and my vision blurs with a red rage-filled haze.

This is the beginning of the end.

2

LILA

"Motherfucker!"

I jolt awake at the fury that envelops me and seems to suck all the air from the room. I roll onto my side and fear slams into me like a sucker punch when I see the blood dripping from Cooper's clenched fist as he pulls it away from the wall.

"Cooper!" Cammi shouts and the noise only intensifies the pounding in my head. "What does this mean? Did they find us? You said they wouldn't find—"

"What do you think?" Cooper snaps at his sister. Cammi flinches at his tone and he takes a step back and I watch in fascination as his temper seemingly leaves his body and his shoulders deflate. "Cam, I'm sorry. I shouldn't have yelled at you. But we both knew that this was a possibility. When we ran…"

Dizziness washes over me and I roll onto my back. I miss the rest of what Cammi and her brother say but that doesn't mean I'm not wondering what the hell they're talking about. Where did they run from? Who do they think found them?

And more importantly, how the fuck does me being attacked tie into it all?

"You're awake." Cammi rushes to my side and Cooper follows behind her but at a much slower pace, as if he's afraid to be near me.

I stare at my best friend, trying to reconcile what I heard with what I know and it's in that moment that I realize, I don't know much. The revelation is jolting and only serves to make me wonder what the hell I've gotten myself into. Images of Cammi and me over the last few months flash through my mind and I realize that I'm making assumptions. Cammi is my best friend and she's one of the best people I know. And Cooper is, well, Cooper. He's always been friendly, even if he is quiet and standoffish at times.

My eyes are drawn to Cooper's fist and I tip my head toward it. "You should clean that up."

Cammi's head whips around and takes in what I'm looking at. Cooper lifts his hands and turns them over several times as if just noticing that he's bleeding. He's holding a piece of paper in one hand and I can't help but wonder what it is.

"It's fine." He drops his hands back to his sides and blood stains his jeans.

"What's that?" I ask, unable to ignore my curiosity.

"It's nothing," Cammi rushes to answer. She glances over her shoulder at her brother and the electric charge that passes between them is startling. When she returns her focus on me, she changes the subject. "Do you remember anything about tonight?"

I sigh and nod, wishing I didn't. Tears burn at the back of my eyes and I swallow past the lump in my throat. "I guess you were right about Drake."

"I wish I wasn't," Cammi insists.

She lifts my hand and my eyes are drawn to my wrists

where the rope burn sticks out against my pale skin. I yank my hand from her grip. I know that there are matching marks on my other wrist and both ankles and as hard as I try to ignore the pain, it's there, threatening to suck me back into the terror that my night became.

"Um… can I get some ibuprofen or something?" I ask.

Cammi rushes to her feet. "Of course."

With that, she leaves to find me something for the pain. Cooper and I are left alone and the oxygen seems to leave the room. We stare at each other, both seemingly trying to outlast the other as far as speaking up and asking questions. Unable to take his scrutiny, I force words past my lips.

"Can I see that note?" When he makes no move to hand it to me, I switch tactics. "When Drake and his friends were… after they…" I glance away and try to pull myself together. When I'm confident I can form a complete sentence, I return my stare to his face. "After the beating they, uh, talked… a lot."

"What did they say?"

I lock eyes with Cooper and see rage swirling in their depths. His shoulders are tense, and I have to wonder what he's seen in his life that he's learned to control his emotions so well.

"I don't remember a lot of it because I was trying to concentrate on something else but the one thing that stands out is when Drake said 'you should be more careful about who you pick as friends'." Cooper's jaw tenses and his face reddens. I tilt my head and study his facial expression, his body language, for several seconds before pointedly staring at the paper clenched in his fist. "Let me see the note."

He looks down at his feet and clears his throat. "I don't think that's a good—"

"I really don't give a shit what you think," I snap. When Cooper's eyes widen at my outburst, I heave a sigh. "Look, I get it. You barely know me but I'm stronger than you think. At least, I should be. Growing up in an MC…" I glance at him and see his eyes narrowing and I assume he's confused. I shake my head before continuing. "Sorry. MC means moto—"

"I know what it means," he growls.

He drops his gaze to the piece of paper in his hand and seemingly having come to a decision, he thrusts it at me. I reach out, tentatively, and pull the note toward me. I smooth out the wrinkles from his angry grip and stare at the words. As it did when Drake issued his warning about being more careful when choosing my friends, my stomach bottoms out.

> **Consider this a warning. Next time, we won't settle for second best. We'll burn your fucking world to the ground.**

As I'm staring at the words, trying to make sense of them, Cammi comes bursting through the doorway with a glass of water in one hand and presumably a few ibuprofens in the other.

"Here's something for the—"

She stops abruptly when she reaches the side of the bed and sees what I'm holding in my hand. The color drains from her face and the glass of water slips from her fingers, bouncing off the carpet. She whirls on Cooper.

"You told her?" she demands, her tone full of fear.

"Tell me what?" I ask, my stare bouncing from Cammi's back to Cooper's face.

The air in the room feels like it's been charged with a cattle prod and a shiver races down my spine at the vibe I'm getting from my best friend and her brother. Neither one makes a move to answer me and suddenly, I'm overcome with the need to escape.

I try to sit up and groan at the pain that radiates

throughout my body. Cooper rushes to my side and wraps an arm around the front of me to ease me back to the bed. When his fingertips graze the skin of my upper arm, a tingling sensation races through me. His eyes lock with mine but neither of us say a word.

When I'm flat on my back, he takes a step away and thrusts his hands through his mussed-up hair. His hands are shaking, and I can't help but wonder if it's from nerves, anger, or if he felt the same thing I did.

I close my eyes and wait for the pain to subside before trying to get them to talk. It takes several minutes, and the room is silent around me. If it weren't for their ragged breathing, I'd think I was alone.

"One of you better start talking," I say without opening my eyes.

"Lila," Cammi begins and her audible swallow follows. I force myself to look at her and when I do, she's looking at her brother, who is pacing the length of the small room. "Maybe I should take you home."

That wasn't what I was expecting. I thought… no, I *hoped* that Cammi would be honest with me. She knows everything about me and it's jarring realizing that I know next to nothing about her. I push myself up on my elbows and wait for the dizziness to pass before speaking.

"I can't go home." I swing my gaze to Cooper and then back to Cammi. "You know how my family is. If they see me like this, things are going to get ugly."

"Things are already ugly," Cooper shouts.

I flinch at his outburst, guilt warring with anger. I brought Drake into their lives and I'm the one who's been beaten. Maybe I should go home and face the music. At least I know that my family can protect me.

"I'm sorry," I say and swing my legs over the edge of the bed. "Just let me clean myself up and I'll get outta here."

"You can't leave." Cammi's tone is sharp but full of fear.

"Why the hell not?" I counter, frustrated at her back-and-forth attitude. I don't like not knowing what's going on and that's exactly what's happening. Between the note and the events of the night, I'm more confused than I've ever been and these two aren't helping. "You won't tell me what that note means so the only thing I know for sure is Drake has an issue with me. I'll leave and you all will be fine."

"None of this is about you."

I whip my head in the direction of the doorway and see Carmen standing there, tears streaking her face.

"Carmen, you should be in bed."

Cooper closes the distance between himself and his youngest sister, putting his arm around her shoulders and attempting to turn her around. She pulls away from him and takes small steps toward the bed, where she sits down next to me.

"She deserves to know," Carmen says to her siblings.

"Carmen, you don't know what's going on so—"

"Vents, Coop," Carmen says pointing to the wall vent.

"Motherfucker!"

Carmen swivels on the bed and locks eyes with me.

"Drake didn't do this to you because of you," she says.

Cooper and Cammi step closer to the bed as if to be closer to their sister. Both seem to hold their breaths while Carmen continues.

"They're after us."

3

COOPER

They're after us.
My heart splits open at the sadness in Carmen's tone as she utters those three words. Between my sister's fear and Lila's curious expression, I feel like I'm suffocating. I whirl away from the females and stride out of the bedroom. Where I'm going, I have no idea. Just anywhere but in the same room with them.

"Cooper!"

Carmen's shout follows me, and I realize that, as long as I'm in the house, I can't escape. It's not like when we were younger and there were nooks and crannies in every room to hide in. The floor creaks under my weight with every step I take, each time the noise hitting me like a bullet.

I yank the front door open without thinking about what could potentially await me on the other side and stumble out onto the porch. I suck in the crisp night air as I lean against the railing and hang my head. How did this happen? How in the fuck did they find us?

Small feet, with sparkly red toes, enter my line of vision and I raise my head. Lila's battered face stares back at me.

My body instantly reacts to the bruises, my muscles bunching under my shirt. I flex my fists at my sides, trying like hell to calm the rage inside of me. Lila tilts her head to the side as if trying to figure me out.

"You shouldn't be out here." My tone is gritty, commanding.

"Why not?" she asks and takes a step toward me.

Instinct has me trying to back away from her but the railing digs into my back, reminding me that I have nowhere to retreat to. I shove my hand through my hair and take a deep breath. Lila is going to be the death of me.

That could very likely be true.

"Cooper?" She takes another step toward me. "Why shouldn't I be out here?"

My control snaps. "Because it's fucking dangerous," I shout before I remember that we're outside and I have neighbors that I probably shouldn't wake up.

"What's dangerous?" she presses. "Whoever it is that's after you?" Another step forward. "Or you?"

I would have sworn it was impossible for me to be even more tense than I already was, but I'd have been so wrong. Not only do my muscles feel like they're going to snap, but my dick is also trying to start a damn party in my pants. And it's all because of the little sprite in front of me.

"Both," I say, hoping that she's scared of at least one of those things.

"Oh." She hangs her head as if thinking about what that one word means. When she looks at me again, her gaze shifts to my bicep, and her eyes light up. "Does your tattoo mean what I think it means?"

I absently rub my arm, touching the last link, other than my sisters, to my past. As it always does when I think about my ink, my stomach twists in knots. I'm always so careful about keeping it covered but Lila is at our house so damn much that it's impossible to hide it from her. I try to think of an explanation for my tattoo that would convince her that it means anything *other* than what it means.

"What exactly do you think it means, Sprite?" I challenge when I can't come up with anything.

"I think it means that you're part of an MC."

I say nothing in response. What can I say? I sure as shit can't tell her that yes, that's exactly what it means. She's used to a do-gooder club, not the one-percenter kind that I grew up in.

"What I don't understand is why you hide it? Why has Cammi never said anything? Or Carmen? Because I gotta tell ya, I didn't think either of them was good at lying but clearly, I was wrong."

I know I can't answer her questions, but I want to. Especially since, whether I like it or not, she's in danger because of me. Hell, her face is evidence that anyone can get to me, to my sisters, at any time.

I push off the railing and step around her. Before I go inside, I look over my shoulder. "Let's get inside. We could all use some sleep."

Her sigh washes over me as I step through the door. What I wouldn't give to have her sighing for a whole other reason. I remind myself that she's barely legal and Cammi's best friend. Lila is so far off-limits that someone should do to me what I did before we had to run.

"Cooper?"

I glance up and see Carmen and Cammi standing next to the couch, both with expressions filled with fear and uncertainty.

"We're fine. I promise." I silently beg whatever higher power is out there to not make a liar out of me. "Carmen, you need to go back to bed." When she opens her mouth to protest, I hold my hand up to stop her. "Please? We'll talk more in the morning."

Rather than arguing like she normally does, Carmen gives a sharp nod and shuffles toward her bedroom. When her door clicks shut, I shift my attention to Cammi and Lila, who is now standing next to her.

"Don't even think about demanding that I go to bed," Cammi says with all the attitude I'm sure she can muster. "I'm not some little kid that you can order around."

"What would be the point of ordering you around? It's not like you'd listen." Anger burns like acid in my veins. "Oh wait... you'd *pretend* to listen while lying through your teeth."

"Are you seriously blaming me for this?" Cammi shouts as tears well in her eyes. Her head falls back, and she stares at the ceiling, something she does when she's trying to get her emotions under control. When she returns her attention to me, her eyes are dry and her face is red. "If that's how you really feel then maybe I should—"

"Don't you dare finish that sentence," I bark. I close the distance between us and rest my hands on her shoulders. "Cammi, I don't blame you. I blame myself. I blame our dad. I blame the club. But I'd never place that burden at your feet."

Cammi's eyes search mine, almost as if she's trying to gauge if I'm being honest. Apparently, she believes me, because she looks at Lila and smiles sadly.

"You can have the bed tonight," she says to her friend. "I'll sleep on the air mattress." With that, she stands on her tiptoes and kisses my cheek. "Night, Coop."

I watch as they both walk away. Lila glances over her shoulder every few steps and I resist the urge to call her back. I wanted to reach out and comfort her like I do with my sisters, although for very different reasons.

She's too young, Cooper. She's too good, too innocent.

My cock doesn't seem to give a fuck about her age or

innocence. When Cammi's bedroom door clicks shut, I adjust myself. It's going to be a long night.

I make my rounds through the house, double-checking all the windows and doors. When I'm satisfied that we're locked in tight, I go to my own bedroom and head straight toward the closet. I shove the clothes to the sides and drop to my knees in front of the safe.

The door opens after I punch in the code and I reach in to grab my Glock. The weight of the gun takes me back to the last time I used it. I've fired this gun, and others, many times, but that last time it had consequences that are still being dished out.

I check the clip to make sure it's full before I lock the safe back up and make my way to my bed. I strip down to my boxer briefs and climb into bed, putting the Glock on the nightstand, within easy reach.

With my hands behind my head, I stare at the ceiling. My mind races as I think about everything that's happened in the last few years. Images of my dead parents flash through my brain but when I try to force them away, they're replaced with Lila's prone form lying on my porch. Somehow, that image is worse.

I've made peace with what I did years ago. I did it for all the right reasons and because of my actions, Cammi and Carmen can have a somewhat normal life. Or they could, until tonight.

Unable to quiet the voices in my head, I sit up and lean against the headboard. I need to come up with a plan to deal with this latest development. Part of me recognizes that the safest thing would be to pull up stakes and run. I could close the tattoo shop and take my sisters and we could settle someplace new. There's one glaring problem with that plan. I don't want to fucking run.

What other options do you have?

The only other option is to stay and fight. I've been fighting my whole life so why stop now? So many reasons to run exist, yet I find myself dismissing all of them. And if I'm being honest with myself, it's not just my sisters that I want to fight for. Lila didn't ask to be sucked into our shit but that's exactly where she is. Not only do I have to protect myself, my sisters, and our lives, but Lila is now on that list.

A creak in the floorboards jolts me from my thoughts. I grab my Glock and rush to press my ear to the door to listen for footsteps. My pulse races when I hear them, but they pass quickly. I slowly turn the knob and stick my head out to see the closed bedroom doors to my sisters' rooms and that's when I hear it... the front door opens, and I wait to see if it closes. When it doesn't, I make my way down the hall.

I see a figure pacing back and forth on the porch and I suck in a breath. When the person turns, relief floods my system and I tuck my gun behind my back, into the waistband of my boxer briefs. I shake my head in disbelief. She can't be that stupid.

"What the hell are you doing?" I demand when I reach the doorway.

Lila's head whips up and her nostrils flare. She opens her mouth several times, but no words come out. Instead, her eyes travel from my face, down the length of my body, and back up again.

"Cat got your tongue, Sprite?"

"I... no." She shakes her head.

I chuckle at her obvious discomfort. I know exactly how she feels. I'm just better at hiding it. "Are you going to answer my question?"

"What question?"

"What are you doing out here?"

"Oh, right." She shifts on the balls of her feet and wraps her arms around herself. "I couldn't sleep."

"So, you thought it was a good idea to come out here where you could be seen?" I know I'm being unfair to her, especially after what she's been through, but I can't help the snide comment.

"Look," she snaps and steps toward me to stab a finger at my chest. "I'm not your sister and I'm not a naive little girl. You don't get to question my decisions."

I wrap my hand around hers and pull her closer. "That's where you're wrong," I growl, bending to get in her face. With my mouth inches from hers, I continue. "You're in *my* house, you're my sister's best friend, and you've brought the past back to haunt us. I have every right to question you."

Lila rears back at my words and yanks her hand out of mine. Her eyes are wide and filled with fire. Something about the green depths gets to me on a very primal level. I hate that I put that expression on her face and at the same time, I revel in it. I affect her. Sure, maybe it's just anger but anger breeds passion and passion breeds so many other tempting things.

"I'll be out of here first thing in the morning." Lila practically spits the words at me before turning on her heel and rushing back inside.

I watch her go, instantly regretting how harsh I was. The shit storm that is my life isn't her fault. No, it's my own damn fault for getting too comfortable. And if anything, she's in danger because of me.

I stride inside and lock the door before going back to my bedroom. I put the Glock on the nightstand and sit down on the edge of the bed. I know that, as much sense as it makes, we won't be running. I've created a good life for my sisters and myself and I'll be damned if I'm going to let the actions of my dad ruin one more thing.

Mind made up, I swipe my cell off the nightstand. I punch in the number I memorized shortly after arriving in Indiana and listen as it rings. I'll have hell to pay for sure, in the morning, but I'm out of options. I'm one man and there's no way I can go up against the biggest one-percenter club in Nevada. Besides, it's not just me and Cammi and Carmen. Lila is involved now and there's no way I'll let—

"Hello?"

I have no idea who the deep voice belongs to but if it's not the man I need to talk to, then I'll make them put him on the phone.

"Is this Isaiah?"

4

LILA

"*Is* that what you want, Sprite?"

I stare into Cooper's eyes and tighten my legs around his waist in response. He continues to thrust in and out of me and when he dips his head to tease my neck with his tongue, I can't hold back the moan that escapes me.

My nails dig into his pecs as the tension builds. Cooper leverages himself up and slides his hand between us. When his finger swirls around my clit, my hips buck wildly. I'm no virgin but I had no idea how good sex could be.

"Oh fuck... Holy shit..."

"That's it, Sprite," he whispers in my ear as he increases the pressure of his finger and speed of his thrusts. "Come for me."

I feel as if a firecracker is going to go off inside me at any moment. I throw my head back and savor the seconds leading up to the explosion.

"Where is she?"

I lift my head and stare at Cooper, confusion clouding my lust. "What did you say?"

"I asked you a damn question. Where the hell is Lila?"

Cooper's lips are moving but they don't match the words I'm hearing.

"You've got two seconds to tell me where she is before I—"

The voice finally registers, and I'm jolted awake long before I'm ready. I throw the covers off of me and swing my legs over the edge of the bed. They're shaking and I'm reminded of the dream that was interrupted.

"I didn't call, I promise."

I lift my head and see Cammi standing there, a look of contrition on her face. I absently rub my eyes and cringe when the pain reminds me of the bruises I got last night.

Just as I stand up, Isaiah comes barreling through the door, Cooper right behind him. To my dismay, Tillie is right behind Cooper. I let out a groan and glare at Cooper.

"What the fuck, Cooper?" I demand, certain it was him that called. Cammi may have kept a lot from me but she wouldn't go behind my back like this.

"Don't put this on Cooper," Isaiah snaps. "You should have been the one to pick up the damn phone and call, Lila Rose."

"Oh please." I roll my eyes. "I'm not a damn child." I shift my attention to my sister. "Tillie, c'mon. You get it, right?"

My sister shakes her head and crosses her arms over her chest. "No, Lila, I don't get it. You're hurt and you don't call your family? What the hell is going on with you?"

My mind immediately conjures up an image of the note. I glance at Cooper and then at Cammi. Both seem to be waiting for me to blab their secrets. Not that I could. I don't fucking know anything.

"Bad choice in men." The statement comes out sounding more like a question.

"Yeah, I don't think so," Tillie retorts. "Bad judgment in men doesn't equal a bruised face."

"Since when?" I counter. "That's all it equals, Til. You of

all people should know that." I turn away from her and face Isaiah. "You too, *Pres*. It's what we deal with every single day."

"Which is exactly why I'm not buying it," Isaiah says, his tone screaming frustration.

"Listen," Cooper says. "Let's all calm down and go out into the living room where we can talk."

I glare at him, hoping to convey just how pissed I am that he called Isaiah. Pissed and… hurt. So fucking hurt. Which isn't something I should be feeling because Cooper owes me nothing.

I bend to pick up a discarded hoodie off the floor and tug it over my head. I shove past everyone and head to the living room where I flop down on the couch. It takes a few seconds for them to join me. Cammi is the only one to sit down with me. The other three adults pace the room, anger evident in each step.

"There is so much we need to discuss," Isaiah begins. "But first, I want a name."

"Name?" I ask, pretending I don't know what he means.

"Yes, *Lila*, a name." He sighs and steps up to the couch, the tips of his boots touching my toes. He bends down so he's in my face. "Give me the fucking name of the shithead that did this to you. Now."

I swallow past the lump in my throat. I've known Isaiah my entire life, but he's never scared me before. He's usually pretty even-tempered but ever since returning from the military, he's different. More focused. Unless it comes to my sister and then he's just a big old puddle of stupidity.

"His name is Drake," Cammi responds when I don't. "Drake Stine."

Isaiah takes a step back and pulls his cell phone from his pocket. He taps the screen and puts the device to his ear. When the only words he says are 'Drake Stine' before he returns the phone to his jeans, I know he's called one of the brothers to do some digging.

"Was that really necessary?"

"I'm going to pretend you didn't just ask me that," he responds, sounding exasperated. "Now, talk."

"There's nothing to talk about. I'm fine."

"Your bruises say otherwise," Tillie mutters. She stops pacing and sits on the other side of me. "Lila, why didn't you call me?"

"And tell you what, Til?" I argue. "That I can't possibly live up to the club's impossible standards so I've done everything I can think of to distance myself? That there's more to life than the club? Or that, because of those things, I got my ass beat up by a prick that I thought I was in love with?" I shoot to my feet. "Huh? Which of those things should I have told you?"

"That wasn't your fault," Cooper says from behind me.

I whirl around to face him, crossing my arms over my chest as I do. "That's not what you said last night."

He shoves a hand through his hair, a gesture I'm coming to realize he does quite a bit when he's frustrated. "I didn't mean to imply that it was your fault."

"Could've fooled me."

"Lila, stop." Cammi's voice is quiet, almost as if she's measuring her words carefully. "What happened to you isn't anyone's fault." She faces her brother. "You read the note, Coop. They're after us, not Lila. She couldn't have known who Drake was. Hell, we still don't know who he is. Not really."

Isaiah turns to Cooper. "You keep mentioning a note. I don't remember you saying anything about one when you called. I need to see it."

"No, you—"

"Don't," Isaiah snaps at me. "You're not calling the shots anymore, kid."

"I'm not a fucking kid!" I shout. "I'm not that little girl that followed you all around like a lost puppy dog. I'm nineteen years old. Start treating me like it."

"Start acting like it and maybe we would," Tillie says.

"Both of you," Isaiah barks. "Stop." When Tillie and I both shut our mouths, Isaiah looks to Cooper. "The note?"

"I called you because I thought you should know what happened to Lila." Cooper crosses his arms over his chest and his tattoo peeks out from under his sleeve. "It wasn't an invitation to bark orders at me."

Isaiah's jaw ticks and he's quiet for what feels like forever. When he speaks, it's with steel in his tone. "I don't give a shit *why* you called. You called and this involves my family, not yours. Now," he sticks his hand out, palm up. "Note. Please."

Cooper looks from Isaiah to Tillie and finally, at me. He takes a deep breath and says, "What do you want me to do, Sprite?"

Stunned by the question, my eyes widen and my jaw drops. He didn't give a shit about what I wanted when he called Isaiah, so why does he care now?

"Just show them." I heave a sigh and drop back down onto the couch.

Cooper nods and goes to his bedroom, presumably to retrieve the note. When he returns, he hands it to Isaiah. Isaiah's expression morphs from frustration to rage as he skims the words.

"What the fuck does 'we won't settle for second best' mean?" Isaiah looks to Cooper for a response.

"I'm guessing it means that Lila isn't the real target."

Isaiah seems to think about that while Tillie asks, "Who else would the target be?"

"We're the targets."

The five of us turn toward the hallway to see Carmen standing there. Perfect timing, just like last night. Honestly, I'm surprised she didn't come out earlier, but I don't blame her for wanting to stay out of it.

"And you are?" Isaiah asks, squinting his eyes at her.

"Isaiah!" I snap. "She's just a kid. You don't have to be an ass."

Isaiah's face softens. "You're right. I'm sorry." He returns his attention to Carmen. "I'm Lila's brother." I snort at the term. "What's your name?"

"I'm Carmen. Cooper's my brother."

"It's nice to meet you, Carmen, although not necessarily under these circumstances."

"Yeah, you too." Carmen rolls her eyes and then takes a few steps toward Cooper. "Anyway, Drake and his asshole friends—"

"Language," Cooper admonishes her.

"Well, it's the truth. They're assholes." At Cooper's stern look, Carmen sighs. "Fine. Those dumbas—" She pauses to correct herself. "Those *jerks were* just using Lila to get to us. More specifically, they wanted to get to Cammi because they know that hurting one of us would throw Coop off his game, and then they could get to him."

"Who is 'they'?"

Isaiah asks Carmen this question but it's Cooper who answers.

"Knights of Wrath MC."

5

COOPER

Knights of Wrath MC.
Knights of Wrath MC.
Knights of Wrath MC.

The words rattle around in my brain, bouncing off of every nerve ending that can be linked to emotion like the little metal balls in a pinball machine. There was a time when I thought I'd be a Knight, that I'd never walk away from the club I grew up in, but that was a long time ago. Back before I realized who my dad was, *what* he was. That was before I did what I had to do to make sure that he couldn't hurt anyone else. Before I broke the code of the club to secure a future for Cammi and Carmen.

"Cooper?"

I whip my head to the left and see Isaiah standing there, arms folded over his chest, confusion etched into the lines on his face.

"Who are the Knights of Wrath?" he asks when I don't speak.

How the hell am I supposed to answer that? I glance at Lila and one thing becomes painfully clear: it doesn't matter how I answer. The result will be the same. My secrets will no longer be secrets and I won't be able to continue pretending that I'm any better than the legacy I left behind.

I heave a sigh and scrub my hands over my face. "The Knights of Wrath is an MC in Nevada."

"Why are they after you?"

"It's complicated."

"Uncomplicate it, then." Tillie stomps to my side and grips my bicep in an attempt to spin me to face her. She may be a bit bigger than her sister but not by much, so I don't budge. "Dammit, start talking. My sister was attacked and according to that note, it's because of you. Start talking."

"Tillie, calm down," Isaiah says as he steps up behind her and puts an arm around her shoulders.

"I will not calm down," she counters. "This is Lila we're talking—"

"Exactly!" Lila shouts. "This is about me." Her gaze swings from Lila to Isaiah and then finally lands on me. "It doesn't matter why they're after Cooper." She hangs her head, and her shoulders rise and fall with each deep breath she takes. When she raises her head again, her eyes lock onto her sister. "Look, if it weren't for Cooper, you wouldn't be here. I didn't want you here and this is exactly why. You're just like Dad and Micah and Griffin, just like Mom and Sadie and Brie. You think you can fix everything and that you're always right. Well, I've got news for you… you can't and you aren't."

"Lila, you're wro—"

"You guys don't get it," she huffs out. "You can't protect me from everything. The world is a lot bigger than the Brotherhood and there is evil out there that you can't always see coming."

"True," Isaiah concedes. "But that doesn't mean we can't do everything in our power to try to protect you. It's what we do, Lila. What would your dad say about this? Your mom?"

"If I gave a damn about what they'd say, I'd have let Cammi take me home last night."

"You barely know these people."

"You've gotta be kidding me." Lila's tone is full of outrage. "*These people* have given me a roof over my head, a place to stay when I was kicked out of my apartment." She slams her mouth shut as if she said too much.

"What do you mean you were kicked out of your apartment?" Tillie asks.

Lila sighs dramatically. "This is all stuff you'd know if you weren't so wrapped up in your own shit, in that shelter."

"Lila," Isaiah growls, warning clear in the single word.

The rest of their argument fades away as I lose myself back in my own head. While I can appreciate that the focus has shifted from me and my past, I hate that Lila is being raked over the coals. Can't they see that she just wants a little independence, to be acknowledged as an adult with a brain? Besides, hasn't she been through enough in the last twenty-four hours?

Unable to stay silent, I clear my throat to get their attention. All eyes turn to me. "We're getting nowhere here." I twist to focus on Isaiah. "I called you because I thought you had a right to know what's going on." I hold up a hand to stop him from saying anything when he opens his mouth. "You want answers, I get it. And you'll get them. I promise. But right now, our focus should be making sure that Lila heals up and that we're all safe."

Isaiah appears to think over my words and then nods. "Agreed." He glances at Tillie and then Lila. "While we wait to sort things out, I think it would be best if you came home."

"I'm not going anywhere," Lila says before lifting her eyes

to mine. "I trust Cooper. I'm safe here. Anyway, I've gotta start preparing for next semester."

My heart thuds wildly against my ribs. I don't know what I did to earn her trust, especially now that she knows we've all kept secrets from her, but I'll do everything in my power to keep it. Letting Lila stay here is probably a huge mistake, especially if my physical reactions to her are any indication, but I'll survive. I just have to maintain my distance as best I can with her under the same roof.

"Right, like you were safe last night," Tillie mutters. When Lila only glares at her, Tillie says, "Fine. But at least come to the shelter on weekends. You're gonna need money to find a new apartment, right? You can work there part-time."

"No, I can't." Lila shakes her head. "I, uh, already have a job lined up."

"Oh yeah? Where?"

"Well," Lila glances at me while she speaks. "Cooper offered me a job at his shop."

"I did?" Lila widens her eyes at me, as if to ask me to play along. "Oh, right. I forgot we talked about that the other day."

"See, it's all good," Lila rushes to say before her sister or Isaiah can get a word in edgewise. "Now, please just go."

Lila strides to the front door and opens it as if to shoo them out. Isaiah and Tillie share a look. He's probably hoping it's unreadable but it's not. Not by a long shot. His expression screams 'this isn't over'.

"Cooper," Isaiah sticks out his hand and I shake it. "It was nice to meet you, although the circumstances are shit. I expect to be kept in the loop about this."

"I wish I could say it's been a pleasure but if you keep throwing demands at me, I'm more likely to tell you to go fuck yourself."

I can't help the anger-filled response. I know I should play nice with Lila's family, especially since I have a strong feeling that I'll be seeing way more of them than I want but playing nice was never my specialty.

Isaiah steps up to me, chest to chest, and gets in my face. With narrowed eyes and steel in his tone, he says, "Don't make me regret this. You may come from some badass MC, but this is my territory, my home, and you'll play by my rules. As long as Lila is under your roof, you'd do well to remember that."

He stares at me for a moment longer, no doubt letting his words sink in, before he turns on his heel and grabs Tillie's hand. He practically drags her out of the house, only slowing to kiss Lila on the cheek as he passes her.

Lila rolls her eyes at them and when they're down the steps, she slams the door and rushes out of the living room. The walls seem to rattle with the bang of Cammi's bedroom door and I stand there, stunned.

What the hell just happened? Does someone else now really know about the Knights of Wrath MC? What the fuck will Isaiah do with the limited information he now has?

So many questions and while it might seem obvious that the Knights of Wrath issue should be the one that's forefront in my mind, it's not. Hell no. The one question that plays on a loop has nothing to do with my past and everything to do with Lila.

Did I seriously just agree to let Lila work at my shop?

6

LILA

"That was... interesting."

I hug a pillow to my chest and avoid Cammi's gaze. She followed me to her bedroom and for a few minutes, she simply stood there and stared. I want to rage at her for not being honest with me about who she is and where she came from, but it would be pointless. The cards have been dealt and now we need to figure out how to play the hand.

"And by interesting you mean humiliating?"

"No. That's not what I mean at all." The mattress dips with her weight when she sits next to me. "Lila, I get the whole feeling like you're being treated like a kid thing, but can I give you some advice?"

I turn my head to look at her and see her wringing her hands. Her knuckles are white, and I reach over to pull her fingers apart. We lock eyes for a moment, and I nod.

"You have a family that cares about you, that wants you to be safe and happy. Don't push them away." She pauses and takes a deep breath. "They won't be around forever and when they're gone, you'll wish things could've been different."

I let her words sink in, let them mix and mingle with

everything else swirling in my brain. I know she's right and I can even admit that I agree. My family is pretty great. I know they love me, and I know, no matter what, they'd do whatever it took to make me happy and keep me safe. I just wish they also treated me like what I want matters.

"Can I ask you something?"

Cammi nods. "Sure."

"Why is Cooper Carmen's legal guardian?"

Cammi sucks in a breath and holds it. I watch as her face turns red and when she doesn't release the air, I snap my fingers in front of her face to get her attention. Air whooshes past her lips and she hangs her head.

"Never mind," I rush to say. "It's none of my business." I don't really believe that. I mean, I'm the one with the bruises and what happened is somehow linked to their past, but I don't want to push her too hard. Not when I just got done reading the riot act to my own family about the same thing.

"No, not never mind."

Cammi stands and walks to her dresser, opening the top drawer and pulling something out. Her back is to me so I can't see what it is at first but when she pivots, I recognize it as a wooden picture frame.

She takes a few steps back toward me and stretches out her arm to hand me what she's holding. I take it from her and look at the image behind the glass. A beautiful woman stares back at me from the seat of a Harley. Her arms are wrapped around the man sitting in front of her.

The man is wearing a cut over a white t-shirt and I recognize the bottom of a tattoo on his bicep that matches Cooper's. In fact, almost everything about the man matches Cooper, from the color of his eyes to the dimple on his right cheek and the angle of his nose. They both appear happy, but the woman's smile hints at something else, an emotion that

I've seen all too much in the clients of the Broken Rebel Brotherhood: fear.

"Your parents?" I ask, glancing at Cammi.

"Yeah." She tilts her head toward the picture. "That was before Carmen was born. Before things got too bad."

My gut twists because even though Cammi's never talked about her parents and I don't know anything about their history, I know what's coming. My heart breaks for her, for Cooper and Carmen too.

"Jimmy... uh, our dad, was a patched member of Knights of Wrath, but it was our mom who grew up in the club. Her dad, our grandfather, was the Enforcer and all-around asshole." It's hard for me to comprehend saying that about family but I'm quickly learning that all families are different. "Anyway, from what we were told, our dad was the poster boy for one-percenters. He had a mean streak a mile wide, but he could also be charming, and he supposedly laid it on thick with Mom."

Tears spill over Cammi's lashes and glide down her cheeks. Part of me regrets asking her about her parents but then I remember that, sometimes, talking about things helps. Maybe that will be the case for her.

"Our mom tried to leave several times. She'd pack us all up and load us in the car, but we never got far. One member or another always tracked us down and took us back. She'd married our father, and, in our club, you were loyal, no matter what. You didn't leave. You didn't bitch when things got rough. You sucked it up and stuck it out. There was no other option."

"Aw, Cam, I'm so sorry."

She waves away the platitude as if it means nothing. And I suppose it doesn't mean much to her, other than I care. Too little, too late.

"Cooper took the brunt of Dad's temper. Well, Cooper

and Mom. Carmen and I were on the receiving end sometimes but it was never as bad for us. Maybe it was because we were younger or maybe we just have an amazing big brother who made sure that we were spared more often than not." She raises her head and locks eyes with me. "I suspect it's the latter."

The weight of what she's revealing hits me square in the chest. I rub my fist into my ribcage as if that will ease the pain coursing through me at the thought of what they've all endured. I swallow back the bile rising up the back of my throat and force out my next question.

"What happened to your—"

Cammi's bedroom door swings open and bounces off the wall, startling us both.

"That's enough," Cooper barks, his eyes shooting daggers at me. He steps in front of Cammi and reaches a hand out to her. "Can you give us a minute?" he asks his sister, a forceful calm entering his tone.

Cammi takes his hand and lets him pull her to her feet. She steps around him and leaves us alone in her room. The walls seem to close in around us, his size taking up what feels like more space than usual.

Cooper's arms are crossed over his chest and his feet are braced apart. His spine is straight and his muscles tense. I rise to my feet and mirror his stance.

"What?"

"If you've got questions about our family, ask me." His jaw tics. "Don't bring it up to Cammi again. Got it?"

"Why?"

"Does it matter?"

"Well, yeah, it does." I drop my arms to my sides and take a step forward. "In case you've forgotten, Cammi is my best friend. I care about her and would never do anything to hurt her. But Cooper, she's nineteen. Seems to me she can tell me to fuck off if she doesn't want to talk about it."

Cooper tips his head back and stares at the ceiling, his chest rising and falling with each breath he takes. When he looks at me again, his eyes seem to swirl with concealed rage.

"If you've got questions, ask me," he says from between clenched teeth.

"Fine." I narrow my eyes at him. "What happened to your parents? And why are you on the run from the Knights of Wrath?"

"They're dead and none of your business."

Cooper turns to walk away but I reach out and latch on to his shirt to stop him. He slowly turns his head to glare at me, but I stand my ground. When he raises one brow at me, I do the same, my stubbornness coming out in full force.

"Let go," he commands.

"No."

A growl rumbles out of him, no doubt his way of trying to scare me into doing what I'm told, but it has a very different effect. One I'm certain he doesn't want from me.

"You don't scare me."

"I should."

I let go of his shirt but rather than step away, I move closer. "Why's that?"

The question comes out huskier than I intended and his nostrils flare. He finally turns back to face me, straightening his arm out to wrap his hand around the back of my neck. Cooper urges me forward. I don't resist and when our noses are so close they almost touch, my breath hitches.

"Because Sprite." He leans in and his breath skates across my ear as he whispers three words that turn my world upside down.

"I'm a murderer."

7

COOPER

Seven years earlier...

"When are you gonna be home?"

The screaming in the background almost drowns out Cammi's question. Between that and her crying, I haven't been able to get much information out of her other than Dad's on one of his tirades.

"Cam, where's Carmen?"

My mind races with the possibilities. I don't normally leave the girls or my mom home alone but Carmen and Cammi were in school and it's Mom's birthday. I wanted to surprise her with a gift because I knew Dad wouldn't. I thought I had enough time, especially with Dad out on a run for the club. Apparently, I was wrong.

"She's right next to me." Cammi sniffles and my heart beats against my ribcage like a marching band drumline. "We're scared, Coop."

"I know and I'm on my way." I need to find a way to keep her on the phone and not kill myself in the process while I race for home. I remember that I have my Bluetooth and reach in my saddlebag for it. When my fingers curl around it, I shove it in my ear and connect it to the cell that's now in my pocket. I don't make a habit of being on my cell while riding my Harley, but this situation calls for an exception. "Can you get to your bedroom, Cam? Without him seeing you?"

"I… I don't think so," she stutters. "We're in the bathroom and they're in the living room."

Something crashes and the fact that I can hear it over my bike tells me that Cammi and Carmen are closer to the destruction than is acceptable.

"Is the door locked?"

"Yeah."

"Good. That's good." I slow to take the right-hand turn that will lead me to our house on the outskirts of town. "Here's what I want you to do. Are you listening?"

"Uh-huh."

"I want you to lift the lid off of the toilet tank. Can you do that?"

"Yeah, hold on." Shuffling noises drift through the line and then the clank of porcelain. "Okay, got it."

"Good. Now, do you see the gun that's taped to the inside of the tank?"

"Cooper, no," Cammi whines. She hates guns and is generally afraid of them. Unfortunately, she doesn't have the luxury of being afraid right now.

"Cam, I need you to get the gun. C'mon, now. You can do it."

"I don't wa—"

"Cammi, now!"

Again, she sniffles, but she doesn't argue. "I've got it."

"Good job." I know she's not going to like this next part, almost as much as she didn't like getting the gun. "Now, I need you to set the cell phone down next to the crack between the door and the floor." When she starts to protest, I speak over her. "I need to hear what's going on. Once you set the phone down, you and Carmen get in the tub and lie down. And you stay there until you hear me or mom at the bathroom door. You got it? You don't move for anything or anyone else."

"O-okay."

"Cammi, if anyone other than mom or I tries to come into the bathroom, you pull that trigger. Got it?"

"Cooper, I—"

"Promise me," I snap. "I know you don't want to, but this is why I taught you how to shoot. So you could protect Carmen and yourself."

Cammi's sobs come harder but she pulls herself together somehow. "I promise, Coop."

"Okay. Great." I take the last turn onto our road. "I'm almost there. Now put the phone down so I can hear what's going on."

"Okay." There's rustling, like she's doing what she's told, but then her small voice comes through the line again. "I love you, Coop."

"Love you, too, Cam."

Finally, the phone hits the floor with a thud and the fight in the background intensifies. I grip the handlebar tighter and trees whiz by as I fly down the road.

"You stupid fucking bitch!" My dad's voice is booming.

"Jimmy, please," Mom pleads.

"'Jimmy, please,'" Dad mocks her in an enraged sing-song voice. "How many times do you have to be told to…"

His voice fades away when I turn in our driveway and skid to a stop. I toss my cell to the ground, not giving a shit if it breaks. I take off running up the walkway, their screams penetrating the walls and making the hair on the back of my neck stand up.

"Jimmy, no."

I barrel through the door and it bounces off the wall at the same time the shotgun blast goes off. I watch in horror as my mom falls to the floor in a heap. Her face is unrecognizable and the lunch she made me earlier makes a reappearance as I drop to my hands and knees and puke.

"Where the fuck were you?"

I slowly raise my head and swipe my mouth with the back of my hand. My vision blurs as I struggle to my feet and stare at the man who calls himself my father.

"I asked you a question, boy."

Spittle flies from his mouth as he yells. When I don't speak, he stomps toward me and grabs me by the hair. My scalp stings when he yanks me away from the doorway and slams the wooden barrier shut, making me wish I'd listened to him the many times he demanded I cut my hair.

I catch a glimpse of my mother's dead body and instantly that wish disappears. I manage to get to my feet and as I straighten my spine, I slide my knife from its sheath in my boot. I'm now towering over him, thanks to a growth spurt last year, but it doesn't faze him.

We stare each other down, him with the shotgun at his side like he doesn't have a care in the word, and me gripping my knife, ready to strike at any moment.

"What the fuck are ya gonna do with that thing? Haven't I taught you better than that? You never bring a knife to a gunfight."

"Is that right?"

"You know it is," he sneers. "Besides, anything happens to me and you're done. The club will kill you *and* your sisters."

I lunge at him and he jumps back with a laugh, narrowly avoiding the blade. He hops from one foot to the other, like a boxer in the ring avoiding a match-ending blow.

"Don't you dare threaten them, old man," I snarl.

"Or what?"

"You don't wanna know."

He steps toward me, still not raising the shotgun. He's a cocky motherfucker but what he doesn't know is his time on this earth is up. The second he squeezed the trigger and killed my mom, his life ceased to matter.

"C'mon, boy," he taunts. "You think you're gonna be their savior? Hell, you couldn't save her so what makes you so sure…"

The rest of his words fade away as white-hot rage bubbles through me. He glances over his shoulder at the body on the floor and that's when I launch myself at him and thrust the knife into his flesh. He tries to fight me off but I'm bigger than him now, stronger.

We crash to the hardwood and I manage to roll us over so I'm straddling him. I pull the blade out of his side and blood drips from the tip.

His eyes are wide, almost as if he didn't believe I'd actually stab him. His hand automatically goes to his wound and when he brings his fingers in front of his face, they are covered in red ooze. His bloody sneer morphs into a dry laugh.

"Go ahead," he gurgles, the laugh dying in his throat. "Kill me."

That's exactly what I do. I stab him, over and over, making sure to pierce his lungs and heart. I let years of abuse and fear and rage flow out of me, through the knife, and into him. I have no idea how many times I thrust the knife into his body but eventually, my arms weaken.

My chest heaves as I struggle to breathe. Pushing myself off of him, I fall to the floor by his side. Blood soaks my clothes, but I don't care. He's dead and that's all that matters.

It's finally over. His earlier warning about the club coming after me, Cammi, and Carmen filters into my thoughts and it's as if someone dumps a bucket of ice water on me.

I scramble to my feet and rush to the bathroom, banging on the locked door.

"Cammi, it's me. Open up." The only sound coming from inside is crying. I pound harder. "C'mon. I need you to open the door."

I hear footsteps on the linoleum bathroom floor and the unmistakable sound of a gun being cocked. I stiffen and send up a silent prayer that I'm hearing things. The door slowly opens, and I make sure that my face is visible in the crack so Cammi can see it's really me.

"Put the gun down," I instruct and gently ease myself into the bathroom.

Cammi stares at me and for a moment, I don't think she's seeing me, but she quickly drops the gun and launches herself into my arms. Carmen is right behind her and I pick them both up and hold them tight.

I was so wrong about it finally being over. The truth is, it's all just beginning.

8

COOPER

Present day...

I park the car in the lot behind the rented space where my shop, The Ink Spot, is located and sit there for a few minutes, hoping the image of my dead mother fades. When it does, I swing the driver's door open and climb out of the car. The hair on the back of my neck shoots up like tiny little soldiers standing at attention.

Turning in circles, I search for the cause but find nothing. There are several other cars, all of which I recognize. The Ink Spot is in an old strip mall and the only other business still in operation is Sandy's Lingerie and Gifts. There's not much crossover between their customers and mine but the women who work there are friendly and have always made me feel like a welcome addition to the building.

"Hey, boss." Beth, one of only two employees I hired when I first opened, is standing with her hip propped against the counter and her fingers wrapped around a mug. "Coffee's fresh."

"Thanks. I'll get some in a minute."

I stride past her and into the broom-closet sized room I call an office. I kick the door shut behind me and drop my bag on the rusting metal desk. I pull out the artwork I drew up over the weekend for my first client of the day and then my laptop. I don't always bring it to work, as I have a desktop already, but I want to do some digging on Drake and didn't want anything linked to my work computer.

A knock on the door pulls my attention. "Come in."

The door swings open before the words are even out of my mouth. Donovan, my other tattoo artist, steps just inside the space and grins.

"You know she likes you, right?" he asks, hitching a thumb over his shoulder.

"Who?"

"Who do you think?" When I continue to stare at him, he shakes his head and chuckles. "You really are oblivious. Geez, Beth. Who else?"

"In case you haven't noticed, she's a bit too young. Even if she weren't, I don't date employees."

And that fact brings to mind another woman who's too young and off-limits. Just thinking about Lila sends blood straight to my cock.

"Right. So, does that mean I can take a run at her?"

I narrow my eyes at him. I don't really give a shit who he dates or fucks, but I hate drama and won't tolerate it in my shop. My only two staff hooking up can equal nothing but drama.

"I can't tell you what to do on your own time but while you're on my dime, keep it professional."

"Sweet." He rubs his hands together like some greedy kid who just got handed the golden ticket.

"Anything else?" I raise a brow at him.

"No." Donovan spins around to leave but stops and looks

over his shoulder. "I meant to ask… did you hire another artist?"

Shit! I forgot about that.

"I'm making a final decision today."

"Great. This week is booked solid. It'll be nice to get some fresh blood in here."

With those parting words, he walks away, leaving the office door open. I glance at my laptop and sigh. Might as well prep for the first ink of the day. I can search for info about Drake later.

I spend the next hour finalizing the drawing for my client and when he arrives, he's thrilled with the design and I get started. The design isn't too large, but the intricate detail means I'm sitting in the same position for hours. By the time I'm done, my muscles are screaming at me to move around and stretch.

"Ready to take a look?" I ask, although it's a stupid question considering the guy is practically bouncing in the chair as I wipe off the new tat and apply a thin layer of Aquaphor.

I watch as he rises to his feet and steps up to the mirror, turning slightly so he can see the ink on his upper arm. My heart beats wildly, as it always does in this moment. I know I'm a damn good artist, but my nerves never fail to appear.

"Damn, man," he says with awe in his voice as he stares at the half skull, half Native American head with a full headdress. "This is incredible."

"Thanks." I release the breath I was holding. "Glad you like it."

"Like it?" He turns to face me. "This is insane, dude. I wanted to honor my ancestors, but this goes way beyond my wildest expectations."

"Great." I pick up the flyer I give to all clients regarding aftercare and hand it to him. Then I grab the clear wrap I use on new tats and make quick work of covering his. "You can take that wrap off in a few hours. Make sure you clean it with antibacterial soap and warm water a few times a day and then apply a thin layer of Aquaphor, or something similar. Everything you need to know is in that pamphlet." I nod toward the paper in his hand. "And if you have any questions, you can always call us here at the shop."

"Thanks. I appreciate it." He reaches into his back pocket and pulls out his wallet. "How much do I owe you?"

"I quoted you two-fifty and your fifty-dollar deposit goes toward that so two hundred."

We walk to the front of the shop so I can cash him out. He pulls a wad of cash, secured with a rubber band, out of his front pocket and peels off two one-hundred-dollar bills and a fifty. For a brief moment, I want to question where he got all of that money, but I keep my question to myself. No one gets that kinda dough legally, at least in my experience, but it's none of my business.

"The extra is for you. Really, dude, incredible work."

"Thanks." I pocket the tip. "We offer a ten percent discount for referrals so make sure to tell people about The Ink Spot. Just make sure they know to mention your name."

He thanks me again before he walks out the front door. I look at the schedule for the rest of the day and notice that I have a few hours before my next scheduled client. Sure, we take walk-ins, but Beth is also free and can handle those. I need to hire another artist and do some digging into Drake.

Back in my office, I flip through the resumes, pulling up the pictures I took of the tattoos they completed as part of their interviews on my computer as I do. Within twenty minutes, I've narrowed it down to two candidates: Kendall and Corbin.

I open up my financial spreadsheets and check the finances of the shop. I'm pretty sure I can afford to hire two new staff but want to be sure. When I started interviews, it was with the intention of only bringing in one new person, but Kendall and Corbin are equally good but at different things. Besides, Kendall also has piercing experience so she can bring another revenue stream to the shop.

Decision made, I make phone calls to both of them and offer them positions. They both accept and we agree that they will start tomorrow. Feeling a sense of accomplishment, I switch gears to focus on the only other matter on my mind: Drake.

I open my laptop and type in the security code, something I set up after running from the Knights of Wrath. I have too much club information that could be very damning and while I already turned most of it over to the cops, there are a few things I kept to myself. Mostly, anything to do with my mother. I didn't feel the need to drag her name through the mud since she was dead.

It takes a minute for the internet browser to load and when it does, I type in Drake's full name and start with that. A link for a Facebook account pops up and I click on that. The image in his profile picture mocks me from the screen and I sneer at it. What the fuck did Lila see in this douchebag?

I scroll through his photos and cringe at the few that include Lila. She looks carefree, with a big smile, in most of them. But there's something else, something that triggers a protectiveness that I shouldn't feel. Her face may say, look how happy I am, but her body language is giving off an entirely different vibe. It's closed off, guarded somehow like she wants to be anywhere but where she is at that moment. Huh.

I move on from Drake's Facebook account. He's clearly an idiot but he's not so stupid that he has anything incriminating in his profile. I return to the search results and click on another link. This time, I'm taken to a news article about a string of break-ins. The article says that the break-ins all took place over a six-month time span and each one was a nursing home. Prescriptions were taken, as well as any valuables that the residents didn't have locked away.

A knock at the door startles me and I slam my laptop shut.

"Come in."

Beth pokes her head in and smiles. "We're gonna order some food. Do you want anything?"

A quick glance at my phone tells me that it's almost three o'clock. My next appointment will be here any minute. I spent way too much time on Drake and still feel like I don't know enough.

"No, thanks. I'm not hungry," I lie.

I'm starving but I don't have time to eat. I'll pick up something for dinner on my way home.

Beth eyes me skeptically but doesn't push it. "If you're sure…" I nod. "Okay."

She backs out of the office and pulls the door shut behind her. I scrub my hands over my face and ignore the fact that my stomach is rumbling, grateful that it didn't do that when Beth was still present.

I flip my laptop open again and close out all of the browsers so I can shut it down properly. I review everything I learned, which isn't much, as I prep for my next client. Drake is a douchebag, and he likes to steal from old people. I briefly wonder what else I'd find in his arrest record but push back the thought, promising myself I'll dig more later.

9

LILA

"Are you sure you don't want me to go in with you?"

I glance at Cammi and force a smile. The wrinkles in her forehead betray the worry she's trying so hard to hide. I know I haven't painted the best picture of my family but really, she has no cause for concern. They aren't going to beat me or anything. But they are gonna be furious, especially if Isaiah and Tillie already filled them in on everything.

"I'll be fine, Cam." I take off my seatbelt and pull the lever to open my door. "I promise."

I step out of the car and slam the passenger door shut. I hear the window and turn to see that Cammi has opened it. I lean in and smile.

"Can you wait for me?" I ask, not knowing how long I'll be able to handle my family and wanting a quick getaway if it gets to be too much.

"Sure thing," she replies with too much cheer. She picks up her cell phone from the cup holder. "I've got some reading to do anyway."

I know she's lying. Classes don't start back up for a few weeks and she hates to read. I appreciate the lie though.

"Thanks."

I back away from the vehicle and stare at the main house over the hood. There was a time when that building was my favorite place to be. Being there meant that I was surrounded by family, by the club. It meant love and safety and home. Now, it means worry, overbearing relatives, and a place that wants to clip my wings so I can't fly away.

My steps are slow, purposeful, as I stride to the front door. I take a deep breath before turning the knob and pushing it open so I can step into the main room. My eyes are immediately drawn to the left, where the bar takes up an entire wall. Isaiah is there, along with my father, and they appear to be deep in conversation.

I walk toward them, assuming it'll only take seconds for them to hear me coming and whirl around, but it doesn't happen. When I'm a few feet away, I stop and try to catch some of the conversation.

"I don't like it," my father complains.

"Neither do I, Aiden, but what else is there to do?" Isaiah takes a swig from the mug in front of him. "Tillie would skin me alive if she heard me say this, but Lila is—"

"I know what you're going to say," my father snaps, although there's little heat behind his words. Instead, all I hear is a wariness that has never been there before. "Lila's an adult and can make her own decisions."

"Exactly."

"She's also my baby girl and I'll do whatever it takes to keep her safe." I roll my eyes at my dad's words. "You may be President but I'm her father."

"True enough," Isaiah concedes. "But you, along with the other founding members, made me President because you knew I could do the job. I need you to trust me on this, Aiden."

"It isn't about trust."

"Yeah, it kinda is." Isaiah stands and pushes his stool under the ledge of the bar. "I won't let anything happen to Lila, but I also won't do anything that pushes her farther away from where she belongs. Here, with her family, with the club."

My father stands, as well, and my pulse races as he shifts to face Isaiah because I know he'll spot me. He doesn't disappoint

"Lila." His gaze shifts between me and Isaiah. "How long have you been standing there?"

Everything in me wants to give a sharp reply but I hold it back as I take in my father. He's always been this larger-than-life figure to me but now he just looks tired and worried and… broken.

"Lila?"

I shake my head clear of my wandering thoughts. "Sorry. Um, just a few minutes."

"I see," Dad says. "I suppose you've got something to say about what you heard." Clearly, he expects me to argue, to give him hell for wanting to dictate what I can and can't do. Well, for once, I'm not going to do that. Not like I usually do, anyway.

"Nope." His shoulders sag as if relieved. "I just came by to see everyone and to grab some more of my things."

The lie rolls off my tongue easily and I'm reminded of all the other lies I've told over the years. A foreign feeling washes over me, and I struggle to identify it. Regret? Sadness? It's neither of those. Regret and sadness I can deal with. No, what I'm feeling is shame and I'm not sure how to handle it.

Rather than even try, I say, "Is that okay?"

When my father doesn't respond, Isaiah takes a step

toward me. "Of course it's okay, Lila. This is your home. You're welcome here anytime." He takes another step forward and rests a hand on my shoulder, leaning in to whisper, "Go easy on him. He's worried about you, but he loves you so much."

Isaiah gives my shoulder a gentle squeeze and then moves past me, leaving me alone with my dad. I shuffle my feet, suddenly feeling like a little kid and nothing like the adult I want them to see me as. I keep my gaze trained on the hardwood floor, unsure what to say.

"Are you okay?" My eyes meet my father's and the concern I see guts me. He tips his head toward my face. "I mean, you're not in pain or anything."

I realize he's talking about the bruises on my face and I suddenly wish I'd taken Cammi up on her offer to cover them up with makeup. I reach up and brush my cheek with my fingertips.

"I'm fine." His eyes narrow and I rush to add, "Ibuprofen helps. And ice."

Dad rocks back on his heels. "Can you stay for a while?" When I open my mouth to respond, he puts a hand up to stop me. "At least for dinner? I'll take you back to your friend's house after. If that's what you want."

"Oh, um, yeah. I can stay." I hitch a thumb over my shoulder. "Cammi's outside, waiting for me. Let me tell her—"

"She can stay too if she wants."

For a moment, I want to agree, but think better of it. No doubt, the club will have a lot of questions about what happened and what I know about Cammi and her family, and I don't want her here for that. Not because I have anything to hide but because something tells me that she doesn't need to be subjected to their inquisition.

"Nah. She needs to help Cooper at his shop later." Another lie that comes too easily.

"Cooper? That's her brother? And his shop is The Ink Spot?"

"I see you've done your homework." The words come out sharper than I intend.

"Where my family is concerned, I always do my homework."

Anger burns like acid and I try to ignore it. Some things never change. I don't know why I was thinking they would... or could. Regardless, I agree to stay the rest of the day and send Cammi a quick text to let her know she can go.

Cammi: Are u sure?
Me: Yep. I'll be at your place later.
Cammi: Call if u need me
Me: Thanks

I stuff my phone into my back pocket and return my attention to my dad. "So, what now?"

"Why don't we head on over to the house and you can see Mom?" He takes a deep breath. "You know that Isaiah is going to call Church while you're here, right? To go over what happened and figure out our next move."

I let out a sigh. "I figured." I cross my arms over my chest in an act of defiance. "You know I don't know much, right?"

"That's what I've been told. But we know quite a bit more than we did the other day. Maybe if we share details, a solid picture will form and then we can act accordingly."

My mind races through the information that I *do* know, along with the information that Isaiah and Tillie got when they showed up at Cooper's house. Recalling the name of the club that Cooper grew up in and the fact that I gave Isaiah Drake's full name, no doubt the Broken Rebel Brotherhood has dug up a lot. Griffin has always been a whiz with information and his son, Liam, is even better.

I resign myself to a long day, one I wasn't fully prepared for when I walked in the front door. Might as well get it over with.

I stretch my arm out and say, "Lead the way."

10

COOPER

"Are you still there?"

When I answered the unknown number, I never dreamt that it'd be Lila's sister calling me. Yet here we are.

"Yeah, I'm here."

"So, will you come?"

I try to recall what she's talking about. When she started talking, the shock took over and I began to imagine every worst-case scenario.

"Cooper?"

"Yo?"

"You'll come to the clubhouse, right?"

Oh, right. She'd invited me to come to one of the Brotherhood's Church meetings to go over what happened to Lila and no doubt to gather as much info from me as they can. I'm not convinced my attendance is necessary but Cammi told me that she dropped Lila off at her place when she showed up at the shop and I find it difficult to pass up the chance to see Lila on her home turf.

"Yeah. Yeah, I'll be there." I glance at the rest of my day's schedule. "What time?"

"Four," Tillie responds. "If you want to bring your sisters, you can. They won't be able to sit in on Church but there's plenty here to do."

I breathe a sigh of relief because I don't want to leave Cammi and Carmen at home alone. I know I can't always be there but when I can help it, I try.

"Thanks. I'll do that."

"No problem. Oh," she pauses and takes a deep breath. "Lila doesn't know you'll be here. We'd like to keep it that way."

The hair on the back of my neck stands up. "Why?"

"I don't think that's any of your business."

I work to keep my temper in check. "That's where you're wrong."

"Oh? Do tell, please."

Her condescending tone makes me want to lash out, tell her she doesn't know who she's fucking with. But then I remind myself that I'm a respectable business owner, the guardian of two girls, and no longer a part of the Knights of Wrath world. Hell, I'm exactly who I always wanted to be… not my damn father.

"Look, I'm not trying to piss you off. It's just…"

"Just what?"

"I think Lila made it pretty clear she wants to be treated like an adult." Never mind the fact that I want to treat her like a grown woman. "Keeping her in the dark about things is not only treating her like a little kid, but also a damn quick path to pushing her farther away."

Tillie lets out a loud sigh and I know I've made my point. It doesn't make me feel any better about the situation but at least I can tell Lila I'm on her side.

She's not gonna give a shit when she sees you.

"You're right." Tillie blows out a breath. "If she asks, don't lie. But don't expect me to offer up the information to her."

"That's your choice."

"Thanks," she says mockingly. "See you in a few hours."

The line goes dead and I pull the phone away from my ear to stare at the screen for a second. I have no idea what I just got myself into, but I guess I should prepare as best I can.

I spend the next hour and a half pulling together all of the info I found on Drake, as well as printing off a few documents that I'm willing to share about the Knights of Wrath MC. There are many things I don't bother with, but I convince myself it's because it's none of the Brotherhood's business and not because I don't want Lila to see any more of the evil I'm linked to.

I leave Beth in charge of the shop and finishing up the new hire paperwork with Kendall and Corbin. It's their first day and they're eager to get started on the actual work but first things first. Cammi decides to hang out at the shop and after she promises to stay put until I get back, I head for the Broken Rebel Brotherhood's clubhouse.

When I arrive, it's clear that they're expecting me because rather than having to wait to be let in, the gates swing open and the guy sitting in the booth gives me a quick wave. The gesture is vastly different from what anyone would have received at the Knights of Wrath compound that it takes me a moment to register that I'm really welcome here.

As I drive over the winding road through the property toward the main house, as Tillie instructed via text, I take in my surroundings. I don't know what I expected but this tranquil country setting wasn't it. It's clear that the Brotherhood values security, as evidenced by the numerous cameras located along the perimeter, the guard's booth at the gate, and the fencing around the many acres.

I park in front of the house and notice several individuals

standing on the front porch. I scan the faces for Lila but she's not there. I recognize Isaiah and Tillie and am also able to pick out Micah due to the strong resemblance between him and Isaiah. There's no doubting that they're father and son.

"You must be Cooper."

The man I suspect is Micah strides down the steps and around the front of my car as I get out. He extends his hand and I shake it.

"And you're Micah."

"How'd you know?" He narrows his eyes with suspicion.

"You look just like your son," I respond and tilt my head in Isaiah's direction.

"Oh, right." Micah chuckles and drops his hand. "Well, c'mon inside and we'll get started."

I follow him up to the porch and am introduced to several other members of the club, along with their wives. I find it odd that the women join us when we go to what Isaiah calls the library and it's even stranger when they sit at the long table.

I'm directed to take the seat at one end of the table and when I do, I take out all of the information I brought, along with my laptop. I'm reviewing the documents when the door flies open and bangs against the wall, startling me from my concentration.

"Sorry I'm late," she says, almost as if out of breath, as she rushes in and toward the table. She practically skids to a stop when her eyes land on me. "What are you doing here?" she snaps.

"I asked your sister to invite him."

A man saunters in behind Lila and steps up beside her, slinging his arm around her shoulder. I stand up from my chair and move toward them, reaching out to shake the man's hand.

"Cooper Long, sir." I introduce myself when Lila continues to stand there pouting.

"Aiden Winters. Lila's father." After he shakes my hand, he shifts to face the rest of the room. "Let's get things started, shall we?"

"We're just waiting on Griffin and Liam," Isaiah says from the head of the table. "They were making copies of all the information they found for everyone. They should be here any—"

"We're here," the younger of two men says as they walk through the door.

"Good."

Lila and Aiden make their way to their seats and everyone else gets settled.

"Thank you everyone for coming. This is gonna be a long one, so I suggest you get comfortable." Isaiah looks to the older of the men that entered last. "Griffin, can you pass those copies around while we all introduce ourselves? I know it's not the norm, but we have a guest."

"You got it."

"Great. I'll start." Isaiah looks at me. "We've met but just in case you forgot, I'm Isaiah, President of the Broken Rebel Brotherhood."

By the time it's my turn, the names start to run together. Tillie, Aiden, Griffin, Sadie, Liam, Isabelle, Brie, Doc, Jace, Noah, Adam, and a few more I've already forgotten.

"Wow, okay." I lean forward with my elbows on the table. "I'm Cooper. Uh, my sister, Cammi, is Lila's best friend." I take a deep breath and blow it out slowly. I'm sure there's more I should be saying but until I know for sure what they know, I stay quiet.

"I've also been living at Cooper's house for the last few months."

Lila, it seems, has no such reservations. All eyes turn to

me and several of the faces register a slow burn fury while others simply give off expressions of curiosity.

"I think this is also a good time to mention that Cooper has ties to a one-percent club based in Nevada." Isaiah crosses his arms over his chest. "The Knights of Wrath MC."

"Holy shit," Jace exclaims. "I've heard of them." He twists in his chair to stare at me. "I grew up in Goldfield."

I recognize the town and can't help but wonder what Jace has heard about the KWMC… or me.

"Then I imagine you know how dangerous they are," Isaiah comments.

"Were."

Isaiah's head swivels in my direction. "What?"

"How dangerous they *were*." I rise from my chair. "That chapter of KWMC has been defunct for several years."

"If I'm not mistaken," Aiden begins as he stands as well. "The MC is still dangerous as hell and active somewhere. At least based on the note that was left on my daughter after she was beaten."

I inwardly wince at the barely concealed fury in Aiden's tone. Unfortunately, he's right. And as much as I want to pretend that the KWMC can't hurt anyone anymore, clearly, I'm wrong.

"Right, the note." Isaiah passes around a copy for everyone to see. "It's not clear that it's the KWMC that's responsible for it but it would be pretty damn stupid of us to assume otherwise."

I glance at Lila when the note reaches her. She tentatively grabs it and then drops it on the table in front of her, as if simply holding it will cause her physical pain. The color drains from her cheeks and I realize that I want to go to her, wrap her in my arms to keep her safe. I don't, of course. I can't. Not now, not ever.

I clear my throat. "Look, there's no denying that this is

bad. But it's my problem. I understand that one of your own got hurt and I know there's nothing I can do to make that right." I run my fingers through my hair. "But I'll handle it."

"Cause that's worked out well so far," Tillie huffs out. She looks at Isaiah and shrugs. "I'm sorry, but this is ridiculous. We're seriously sitting here arguing about how dangerous the people that beat Lila are. They beat her. They're dangerous. End of story."

"No, not 'end of story'." Lila stands and makes her way to stand near my chair. "All of you want to blame Cooper and his... association. But what happened to me is on me. Not him. I'm the one that went to Drake's apartment that night. Hell, I'm the one that *dated* him. I'm the one who wanted to live a life outside of the Brotherhood. I'm the one that told lie after lie about where I was, what I was doing, who I was with. *Me*."

Silence fills the room and it's deafening. I stare at Lila and take in her words. I'm amazed that she doesn't blame me like she should, but I'm also grateful and recognize it for what it is. An opportunity. A chance to fix the situation.

"I appreciate the vote of confidence, Sprite."

I reach out and push a lock of hair behind her ear without thinking. Lila's eyes widen at the gesture and I yank my hand back to shove it in my pocket. I don't look away from her, I can't. Her pupils dilate and her nostrils flare.

Fuck! She feels what I—

"Can we get back on track?" Isaiah barks from his spot.

Lila and I both refocus our attention on the matter at hand but the bulge in my jeans doesn't seem to get the memo. I sit back down and adjust myself under the table. I'm damn uncomfortable but I have a feeling it's going to be a while before I can do anything about it.

"Just tell me what you want to know," I say with a sigh.

"Why did you leave Nevada?" Aiden asks.

I contemplate my answer. I could give them the short, easy version: I killed my father. Or I could give them the longer version that makes me look a little better. At least, I think it will, considering this is a club that's not comprised of criminals.

"The KWMC was known for running drugs and weapons." I glance around the table and make sure to look each person in the eye. "They always managed to stay one step ahead of the police but even if they were caught, they had connections." I take a deep breath before continuing, praying that they believe what I'm telling them. "I was tagging along one day and there was a bust. The DEA convinced me to flip, telling me that if I did, I could take my sisters and we could relocate. I agreed."

"Bullshit!"

Liam's fist bangs on the table, rattling everything. He rises from his chair, lifting a piece of paper and handing it to Isaiah as he does. He points to the middle of the page, indicating what he wants Isaiah to read. Isaiah lifts his gaze and locks eyes with me.

"Care to tell us why this says you killed your father?"

11

LILA

The sign on the building seems to mock me as I stand here, leaning against the Jeep my dad let me borrow when I left the club last night. There's movement beyond the glass front and I easily spot Cooper by the way he walks. I berate myself for that but don't stop staring. It's impossible to look away, much like it was after Isaiah called him out on his lie yesterday.

The shock on Cooper's face flashes in my mind and I can't shake it. By the time church was over, the animosity in the room had diminished but that had only triggered thoughts and feelings that I didn't want to analyze at the time. I still don't but I realize I'm going to have to if my dreams last night are any indication.

"Are you gonna come in or what?"

I'm so wrapped up in my own head that I didn't see Cooper step outside. He's standing on the sidewalk in front of The Ink Spot, arms crossed over his chest. I try to swallow but there's no saliva in my mouth.

"Well?"

I can see his brow arch, even from this distance. I push off of the Jeep and force my feet to move, one in front of the other, until I'm a few feet away from him. He turns and walks inside, leaving me to follow.

"Hey, Lila," Beth says from behind the counter. "Long time no see."

Cammi and I used to come to the shop a lot, back before I started dating Drake. "Yeah, it's been a while."

"I wish I could stay and catch up, but I've got my first client coming in a few minutes." Beth steps around the counter to go to her station, calling over her shoulder, "If you're still here when I'm done, we'll chat."

"Sounds go—"

"She'll be here," Cooper says with frustration. "I hired her."

Beth stops in her tracks and whirls around. Her gaze shifts between Cooper and me, confusion wrinkling her forehead. I catch the glare Cooper shoots her way and roll my eyes. It's his own fault if his staff are confused. He should have told them.

You shouldn't have put him in this position.

"Well, I'm happy he did."

Beth retreats to her station without further comment. Cooper and I remain where we are, staring each other down. I'm the first one to look away, trailing my eyes around the shop, trying to think of something to say but come up empty. And Cooper doesn't seem too eager to break the silence.

"Hey, boss, where do you wa—" I shift toward the new voice and am surprised to see someone I don't recognize. The guy can't be much older than me and he's definitely easy on the eyes. Not as easy as Cooper though. "Hello," New Voice says and brushes his palm on his thigh before reaching toward me. "I'm Corbin."

I paste on my brightest smile and shake his hand, making sure to hold on a little longer than necessary. If Cooper wants to treat me like I don't exist, then I'll pretend like he doesn't either.

"Lila. Nice to meet you."

"You too." Corbin takes a step back and drops his eyes to my chest. I wore the low-cut tank hoping it would catch Cooper off guard, but this'll do. "Hot damn, you're gorgeous."

Heat infuses my cheeks and I know they're turning crimson. "Thanks. You're not so bad your—"

"Did you need something?" Cooper snaps as he steps in between us.

"Oh, yeah, um…" Corbin clears his throat. "Sorry. I just signed for the delivery of supplies and wondered where you wanted everything."

"Have Donovan show you where everything goes." When Corbin says nothing and makes no move to leave, Cooper asks, "Anything else?"

"Nope." Corbin leans to the side so he can see me past Cooper. "See ya around?"

"Absolutely."

"Good." He gives a quick nod and straightens. "Well, I'll, um… I'll get this stuff put away."

"You do that."

When Corbin is gone, Cooper whirls around and glares at me.

"What the fuck was that?" he growls.

I square my shoulders and narrow my eyes at him in a defiant look. "What was what?"

"You know damn well *what*."

"No, I don't."

"Yes, Sprite, you do." He takes a step toward me. "You know exactly what you were doing." Another step. Then another. "Let me make one thing clear." He takes the last step to close the distance between us. Heat is rolling off of him in waves. "I agreed to give you a job to satisfy your family. *I'm* helping *you* out. Not the other way around."

I nod, unable to force words past my lips. Having him so near has sucked all of the oxygen from the room and my lungs feel like they won't expand.

"While you're here, you're on the clock." Cooper leans in and his breath tickles my ear. "Unless I say otherwise." He straightens and grins. "Got it?"

Again, I nod.

"No flirting."

Cooper takes two steps back and I'm able to suck in a breath.

"Unless you say otherwise?" I taunt before I can think twice about it.

"Touché."

"What about when I'm off the clock?" I can't help but antagonize him a little more. I enjoy his reaction too much to stop. I rest my hands on my hips. "Am I allowed to flirt then?"

Cooper's nostrils flare and his muscles pull taut. Something tells me I'm playing with fire but for once, I hope I get burned. Burned by his touch, by his words, by *him*.

"Cooper?"

I tilt my head and wait for him to answer my question. His eyes finally meet mine again and that fire I want is there but it's blazing more than I thought possible.

"You're gonna be the death of me, aren't you?" he asks rather than answers my question.

"That depends."

"On?" He quirks a brow.

I open my mouth and slam it shut again. *Shit.* I have no idea what it depends on. I wasn't expecting him to call my bluff. I may flirt and lord knows I'm no saint but I'm also not as *experienced* as I try to portray.

"That's what I thought." He chuckles. "Sprite, you're so far out of your depth with me. Don't fucking wade in waters that are too dangerous to be in."

"Whatever." The word sounds immature, but I don't give a shit. "What do you want me to do... *Boss?*"

Cooper's jaw tenses at the term and I hold back a laugh.

Who's wading in the wrong waters now?

12

COOPER

I pull into the parking lot and turn off the engine. The only light is from the moon and the one working light post at the edge of the lot. I lean my head back against the headrest and let out a long sigh.

Lila's first day went well, once we got past the whole flirting thing. She fits in and everyone likes her, which is a good thing. But she's a distraction, one I can't afford right now. That being said, she's here because of me and there's no turning back.

My eyes slide closed as I recall my dreams last night. Lila has gotten under my skin and now she's invading my sleep. If I'm being honest, it's not exactly anything new but my dreams have never left me feeling needy and wanting. I've always been able to wake up and forget about them.

Liar.

My cock twitches at the memory of how Lila straddled my hips and slid down my length, taking in all of me. We were a perfect fit, better than I ever could have imagined, but then again, it was my fantasy, my dream, so of course, it was perfect.

A car engine breaks the silence of the dark and I sit up straight and glance around. No other vehicles have entered the lot. Maybe the sound I heard was the universe's way of telling me to snap back to reality.

I open the car door and step out, slinging my laptop bag onto my shoulder as I do. A yawn escapes and I rub my eyes. Between my dreams and getting up way too early to avoid Lila, I'm exhausted. I stroll toward the shop and stop dead in my tracks when I reach the sidewalk.

What the fuck?

One of the windows is broken and the words 'found you' are spray-painted on the brick exterior of the shop. Fury builds, threatening to explode from the inside out. I look toward Sandy's Lingerie almost hoping to see similar vandalism because that would mean that I'm reading too much into the words. I'm not that lucky though.

Surprisingly, the door is still locked but it doesn't matter. The damage will cost me a small fortune to fix but worse than that, we're not safe anymore. I let Cammi and Carmen down. I berate myself for not getting a security system, but I really thought we were safe. Apparently setting up the business under a different name wasn't enough though.

After unlocking the door, something catches my eye, pulling my gaze to the floor. There's a folded piece of paper sticking out from under the toe of my boot and I bend to pick it up. When I read the words, my vision blurs with rage.

next time it'll be your house

"Fuuuck!" I shout into the silence.

I dig out my cell phone and call the only person I can think of: Isaiah.

"You know you can't go home, right?"

The look I shoot Isaiah's way is meant to intimidate him, but he doesn't react.

"Ya think?"

Isaiah had shown up within an hour of my phone call, bringing several guys with him. We managed to get the mess cleaned up and put a plywood board over the busted window but that's about it. I called Cammi and told her to keep Lila from coming in and instructed her to stay at the house and keep the door locked. I didn't give her any details but I didn't need to. She knows when I mean business.

"We've got an extra cabin on the property. We usually keep it empty for prospects, but you can use it for now. At least until we get this sorted out. There are rooms at the main house for any potential club members if we need them."

"Thanks, but no thanks."

Isaiah tilts his head. "Why?"

"Because I don't take handouts. I can take care of myself."

"I have no doubt that's true." He takes a breath, releases it slowly. "But I'm not offering for you. I'm offering for your sisters." My gaze snaps to his. "Yeah, figured that would get your attention."

"Shit," I mumble.

"Look, this is escalating real fucking quick. I don't like it and I know you don't either. But it's not just your stupid ass that you need to be thinking about."

"I know that."

"Do you? Because I'm getting hourly fucking reminders from Tillie that her sister is in danger. I've managed to appease her because I happen to like you, despite all the reasons I shouldn't." At the confused look on my face, he chuckles. "Don't look so surprised. I may not like the situation or some of your, shall we say *history*, but I don't think you're a bad guy. In fact, I think you're a lot like me and my club. You'll do whatever it takes to protect what's yours. You treat people around you fairly and with respect. I like that and I think it's good for Lila."

"That's quite the mouthful."

"Yeah, well, there was a lot of solo time when I was a Seal. I'm making up for all of the times I couldn't talk." He grins and I can't help but like the guy. Or at the very least, appreciate his honesty. "Remind me and I'll tell you all about it sometime."

I know when my options are limited and if I don't want to disrupt Cammi and Carmen's lives more than I have to, taking Isaiah up on his offer is the best choice.

"How many bedrooms are in the cabin?" I ask, giving in.

"Two," he replies. "The girls will have to share but it's tem—"

"I can take the couch."

"Yeah, I kinda figured that would be what you'd do."

"You seem to think you know me so well all of a sudden."

"I know everything I need to know."

"And what did you need to know?"

"That you aren't the kinda guy to cut and run when things get tough. That you take care of your own, although I think I already told you that." He pauses, holds my gaze. "That you're good for Lila and I think she'll be good for you." I open my mouth to speak but he holds a hand up to stop me. "Don't bother trying to deny it. I've seen enough grown men fight like hell against what they're feeling so I recognize it. And they all have one thing in common."

"What's that?"

"They lose the fight, every time."

"There's nothing between us," I insist, uncomfortable with the direction the conversation took.

"Denial will get you exactly where you are."
"Huh?"
"Alone."

13

LILA

"Would you stand still?"

Cammi and Carmen are both sitting on the couch as I pace circles around the living room. It's been several hours since Cooper called, according to the time Cammi's given me each time I ask.

"He didn't say why he wanted us to stay put?"

"No, he didn't." Cammi gets up and steps in front of me, wrapping her fingers around my biceps to hold me still. "He'll be home soon, and he'll fill us in."

I pull away from her and continue to pace. Cammi sighs and flops back down next to Carmen. I want to believe Cammi, to have her confidence that Cooper will give us details, but I simply don't. None of them were very forthcoming with information until they were forced to be, and I can't help but think this will be more of the same.

"Maybe you should call him," I say but don't look at her.

"I've called him six times and he hasn't answered." Before I can say anything, she adds,

"And he hasn't responded to the texts either. Lila, calm down. He'll be here soon."

As if on cue, the sound of a car engine filters through the walls, and I rush to the window to pull back the curtain. I watch as Cooper parks and gets out of the car but then another sound reaches me. One I'm all too familiar with. Motorcycles.

"You've gotta be kidding me."

I unlock the front door and barrel out onto the porch just as Isaiah, Liam, and Noah pull into the driveway and park next to Cooper.

"What the fuck are you doing here?" I yell as I descend the steps.

"I invited them," Cooper responds even though I wasn't talking to him.

"Why would you do that? If you want me to leave all you had to do was tell me. You didn't have to bring them to whisk me away." My eyes start to burn so I take a deep breath to calm myself. "Jesus, Coop. I thought you were cool with me staying here. Just because I flirt with a guy… that's what this is about, right? You're pissed about yesterday so you're kicking me out."

"Lila, calm down and give the man a chance to talk."

I glare at Liam, but he doesn't back down. The three brothers are standing there with their arms crossed over their chests, watching me make a fool of myself.

"Go fuck yourself, Liam," I snap.

"Lila?"

"And you…" I march toward Isaiah and stab a finger into his chest. He raises his eyebrows but otherwise doesn't react. "Go tell your *girlfriend* that she needs to back off. Better yet, grow a pair and stand up to her."

"Lila?"

I whirl on Noah. My anger is riding me hard and I don't see an end in sight.

"Noah, I don't have anything to say to you other than be

careful where you toss your loyalties. These assholes will—"

"Sprite!"

"What?!" I shout as I spin around to face Cooper.

"Dammit, woman. Stop yelling at them." He glances up and down the street. "We don't have an audience yet and I'd like to keep it that way." He steps toward me and his face softens. "I need you to listen to me, okay? Are you listening?"

"Yes." I nod

"Good." Cooper cups my cheek. "I'm not kicking you out."

The fury that had taken over dissipates like a balloon that hisses out all of its helium.

"You're not?"

"No, Sprite, I'm not." He wraps his arm around my shoulders. "Let's go inside and we can all talk."

"If you're not kicking me out, what are they doing here?" I tip my head in the guys' direction and stand my ground.

Cooper picks me up and tosses me over his shoulder like a sack of potatoes. I hear the asshole amigos laughing and lift my head to glare at them. It's not lost on me that I'm not at all intimidating in this position, but I try my best.

"I tried being nice."

Cooper's voice rumbles and I can feel the vibrations against my cheek. I want to argue, lash out, scream, do anything other than dangle over his shoulder. Anything other than focus on the way his palm rests on the back of my thigh, just beneath my ass, or the way his fingers are inches away from discovering how wet he makes me.

"I'd ask what she did but I'm sure even residents in the next county know."

Cammi's shoes come into my line of vision just after we cross the threshold into the house. Cooper lifts me off his shoulder and sets me on my feet. Dizziness washes over me at the sudden rush of blood from my head but he steadies me

83

when I sway and doesn't let go, even when I'm able to stand still and straight.

"Now, let's start off with a recap." Cooper bends at the knees and locks eyes with mine. "I'm not kicking you out. Got it?"

"Got it," I mumble.

"'Bout time." Cooper steps back and straightens to his full height. "I invited them here. I get that you don't like it but too bad."

"But—"

"I'm not done," Cooper barks, and I press my lips together like a petulant child. He takes a deep breath. "When I got to the shop this morning, one of the windows was busted and there was graffiti on the wall." I hear what he's saying but I can't help but wonder what he's leaving out. "The details aren't important. Suffice it to say, we're not safe here."

When Cooper stops talking, I exchange a glance with Cammi. I expect to see fear in her eyes but all I see is anger. And maybe a hint of sadness. Isaiah seems to sense that more needs said to ease a few minds.

"You aren't going too far. Just to a cabin on our property. And it's temporary."

"Yes. It is," Cooper adds as he faces his sisters. "I promised you both that you'd never have to worry about them finding us." He drops his chin and stares at the floor. "I'm so sorry I didn't keep that promise."

Carmen rushes to Cooper and launches herself at him. He catches her easily, despite him seeming to have not been paying attention. He wraps his arms around her but when Cammi steps up to his side, he extends one arm to include her.

"It's not your fault," Carmen says quietly.

"She's right," I say, wanting to ease the pain I see etched in the lines of Cooper's face. "You did everything right, Coop. *Everything.*"

He lifts his head and looks at me with glistening eyes and it almost knocks me on my ass. This man who has always been a bit of a hardass, who can give way better than he can get, who plagues my thoughts and fantasies, and my every breath, is losing his shit because he feels like a failure. It's almost more than I can bear.

Cooper sets Carmen down and kisses the top of her head. He pulls Cammi closer and does the same. Somehow, that gesture seems to be what grounds him, infuses him with whatever he needs to move past the pain.

"I need you both to go pack as much as you can. At least what you'll need for a few weeks."

Cammi and Carmen leave the room without any further conversation. I admire the faith they have in Cooper. Hell, I have the same faith. What I don't have is faith in my own family to let me come home but still live my own life.

"What about me?" I ask, not sure I want the answer.

"You're more than welcome to stay with Tillie and me," Isaiah responds. "Or I'm sure your parents would love to have you back in your old room." He pauses and smiles. "But if that's not what you want then I'm guessing—"

"You can stay in the cabin with us." My heart beats frantically. "I told you I wasn't kicking you out and I meant it. It'll be a bit more cramped, but we'll make it work."

I look from Cooper to Isaiah and am shocked when Isaiah grins and gives an almost imperceptible nod.

"Yeah, sure." I swallow past the lump in my throat. "Um, thank you."

"Don't mention it."

14

COOPER

"Can't sleep?"

I swirl the amber liquid in my glass and continue to stare off into the distance, not bothering to acknowledge Lila's question. Nothing but woods and fields surround us, but I know the fence is there and the cameras. When we arrived, Isaiah had taken me on a tour of the grounds, pointing out all of the security measures that the club has in place. It wasn't necessary but I appreciate that he took the time.

Lila brushes up against me and my body responds instantly. My dick swells behind my sweats and my pulse races. I glance at her out of the corner of my eye and take in the way the cool night air pebbles her nipples, the way the flimsy fabric of her tank leaves nothing to the imagination.

I shift away from her, to my left, but she follows, not allowing me to break contact for long. I lift the glass to my lips and down the remaining contents, savoring the burn. I should've brought the whole damn bottle outside.

"Can I ask you something?"

Lila's voice is soft, almost too soft to be heard over the

breeze and the sway of the leaves. I turn so I'm facing her and lean my elbow on the railing.

"Sure."

I know I may regret giving her permission but it's better if we're talking. At least then I'm not focusing on the way she feels up against my body.

"Do you really think I'm in danger?"

Not at all what I was expecting. And I'm not sure how to answer other than with complete honesty. "I don't know."

"What about you? What about Cammi and Carmen?"

"Yes."

"Are we safe here?"

"There's always safety in numbers."

"Yeah, I guess."

Lila shifts and stares straight ahead. I watch as her facial expressions change and her lips barely move but they do move, almost like she's talking to herself.

"What's really on your mind, Sprite?"

She glances at me for a split second. "Nothing."

"I don't believe you."

I lift my hand and rest it on her shoulder. She flinches but it's not from fear. No, it's something else. Something she doesn't want to admit. Shit, I get it because I'm doing the same damn thing.

"Can I ask you something?"

A snort escapes her, and her hand flies up to cover her mouth. "Sorry," she mumbles from behind her fingers. "I don't know why that struck me as funny."

"No need to be sorry," I assure her. "But can I?"

"Shoot."

"What did you see in Drake?"

I'd promised myself a hundred times I would never ask her that, but I have to know. I've found nothing good about him and if I'm reading any of her signals right, she's into me, and I'm the farthest thing from the kind of man—correction, *boy*—Drake is.

"You really want to know?" she asks.

"No, but I *have* to know."

"I don't know." Lila shrugs. "He was cute, fun... for the most part. He was nothing like every other guy I knew, every guy I grew up around."

Her answer both annoys me and makes me hopeful. Maybe she doesn't see me like she did Drake after all. But seriously? That's it? He was cute, kinda fun, and different?

"Lila, you're a smart girl. There had to—"

"Woman."

"What?" I scratch the side of my nose.

"You heard me."

"Fine. You're a smart *woman.* There had to be more that drew you to Drake."

"I don't know what to tell you, Coop." She shrugs again.

"I think you do."

Lila turns and leans back against the railing, crossing her ankles. The stance pushes her chest out and when I look away, I'm captivated by her tan, slender legs. I can't help but wonder what they would feel like around my head. When she drops her head back, exposing her neck, I have to force myself to concentrate on her words and not how badly I want to mark her.

"I never really dated, ya know? My family... over-protective doesn't begin to cover it." She lets out a weak laugh. "I guess I went a little wild."

"A little?"

She rolls her neck and looks at me through narrowed eyes. "I don't expect you to understand."

"I understand more than you think, believe me."

Lila straightens and faces me. "I doubt it."

"I grew up as an unwanted shadow to the worst criminals

in Nevada. I was groomed from the time I could walk to be everything I hated. My father was an abusive prick, and my mother was too weak to stand up to him. I fucking killed to get away from that."

I shove away from the railing and pace the small deck. I can feel Lila's eyes on me, boring a hole into my head like a heat-seeking missile. It takes everything in me to keep pacing and not react.

"Would you stop? Please?"

I don't. I won't. I *can't*.

"Cooper, talk to me." I spare Lila a quick glance but keep walking. "C'mon. It's not like you're telling me something I didn't already know."

My control snaps and I stalk toward her, boxing her in with my arms on either side of her body. I lean in as close as I can get without actually touching her.

"You don't know shit," I growl.

"I know everything I need to know."

The words are so reminiscent of what Isaiah said and I can't take it anymore. I move my hands from the railing to Lila's face and capture her lips with mine, nipping and sucking. In my head, I'm pleading with her to resist but she doesn't.

Lila presses her small frame into me, and my cock begs to be freed. I slide my tongue along the seam of her lips, and she responds by thrusting her tongue to dance with mine. When I try to pull away, her fingers dig into my ass and urge me closer.

I know this is wrong. I know she's too young for me, too good for me. But at this moment, I'm powerless to stop it. I'm hungry for more of her, all of her.

I lift Lila up and her legs wrap around my waist, grinding her core against my dick in the most delicious way. Her grip on my body is so tight, my hands are free to roam and I run them up the back of her shirt, reveling in the fact that, other than her tank, she's bare.

Lila throws her head back and I latch onto her neck, trailing kisses and nibbling at her pulse point.

"Ah, fuck," she moans.

Hearing her voice, knowing that she wants what I'm offering, has me on fire but somehow, I manage to reign myself in. I break away from her and she slides down my body until her feet touch the wooden deck beneath us. We lock eyes and hers fill but she doesn't let any tears fall.

"Lila, I'm—"

"Don't, Coop." She steps around me and rushes to the sliding glass door. When she reaches the threshold, she pauses and glances over her shoulder. "Just… don't."

15

LILA

"Don't let him get to you."

I toss the clothes I'd unpacked less than twenty-four hours ago back into my suitcase. I can't stay here anymore, not after what just happened with Cooper. The asshole was seriously going to apologize for it, too. Talk about humiliating.

"It's not like I'll be far away, Cam." My smile is fake as hell and she knows it. Fortunately, she doesn't call me out. "My parents' house is just on the other side of the property."

"You leave and he wins."

"It's not a game. Not to me anyway." I give Cammi a quick hug and then extend the handle on my now closed luggage. "Hey, maybe when I find my own place, you can move in with me," I suggest, hoping to change the subject, even if only a little bit.

Cammi snorts. "Yeah, right. Like I'll be able to move out. Cooper will have us on lockdown until all this other shit is sorted out. Besides, like your parents are gonna let you live on your own now."

"They can't stop me. I'm nineteen. It's not up to them."

"We'll see."

"Tell Carmen where I went for me? I don't want her to worry."

"I will." Cammi takes a deep breath, holds it for a moment before puffing up her cheeks and letting the air escape past her lips. "Does he know you're leaving?"

"No."

"Won't you at least talk to him before you go?"

I admire her persistence, but she doesn't get it. Cooper's probably gonna be thrilled that I'm gone. She'll see that soon enough.

"I'll call you later."

I don't wait for her to say anything else and make my way toward the front door of the cabin. Just as I reach for the doorknob, a voice stops me in my tracks.

"Where are you going?"

I glance over my shoulder and see Cooper standing in the doorframe between the living room and kitchen, eyebrows arched, body tense. I want to plead with him to beg me to stay. I want to hear him say he wants me here, needs me here. Hell, I'd settle for anything other than 'I'm sorry' or demands about what he thinks is best for me.

When he doesn't say anything, my shoulders sag with disappointment. "None of your business."

I twist the knob and leave, pulling the door closed quietly behind me. I set out to walk to my parent's place, the half-moon lighting my way. A lot of girls would be terrified to walk in the dark on such a vast property but not me. I know this place backward and forwards, inside and out.

I make it a few hundred feet away before I hear yelling, causing me to look back. Cooper and Cammi are on the front porch, arguing with each other. I can't make out their words but there's a lot of pointing in my direction going on so no doubt Cammi's reading him the riot act because I left.

I face forward and force one foot in front of the other. Eventually, I hear nothing but the wind in the trees and the voice in my head chastising me for running because my feelings got hurt. I pull my cell phone out of my pocket and play some music to drown out the voice.

I keep my steps slow in an effort to drag out the walk. I'm not in any hurry to explain to my parents why I'm showing up in the middle of the night. What would normally take fifteen minutes turns into thirty.

When the house comes into view, I'm struck with little flashes of memory, visions of me as a child, running around in the yard or riding my bike. Images of me as a teenager, sneaking out of my bedroom window to go to hang out with Tillie and the guys. Normally, when I think about the past, anger is a foregone conclusion but not this time. No, now all I feel is a sense of home.

The light streaming through the living room window is like a beacon, a reminder that no matter what, I've always got a place to go, a place to belong. Sure, I might face a set of questions that rival the Spanish Inquisition, but the house, the light, like my parents, is a constant in life. Always has been and always will be.

Before I can punch in the six-digit code to unlock the door, it swings open and I find myself wrapped in my mom's arms. I almost resist, pull away and put some space between us. Almost.

"What are you doing up?" I ask when we break apart.

"Funny thing." She urges me inside and shuts the door. The whirring sound of the lock automatically sliding back into place reaches my ears and it's comforting. "Your dad got a text that said you were coming."

"Cammi?"

"Cooper."

I don't know what to say so I don't say anything. Instead, I step around my mom and roll my suitcase down the hall to my old room. I leave it just outside the door and retrace my steps back to the living room and flop down on the couch next to her.

"Wanna talk about it?" she asks.

"Not really."

"Okay." My head swivels and at my shocked expression, she chuckles. "Not what you were expecting?"

"Well, no." I shake my head.

"Honey, I remember what it was like at your age. Nineteen isn't easy. Trying to figure out who you are, what you want out of life, all the while everyone around you is struggling to accept the fact that you're no longer a child."

She breaks eye contact and looks beyond me. I don't have to turn around to know exactly what she's staring at. It's the picture of her standing at the sink in the cabin where she and my dad met. According to my dad, it's the last picture he had of her before she left. She wasn't much older than I am now and based on the stories I heard growing up, she didn't have her shit figured out any more than I do.

"When you're ready to talk, I'm here. I'll always be here."

"Thanks, mom."

She pats my leg and stands up. "Now, go get some sleep. The sun's gonna come up before we know it."

She almost makes it to the hall before I call out to her.

"Hey, mom?"

She looks back. "Yeah?"

"How do you convince someone that they're good enough for you? That their past doesn't matter because all you really see is the good in them?"

"Oh, baby girl, that's easy."

"It is?"

She nods and when she speaks, it's not lost on me that she somehow knew I was talking about a man.

"You show him and make him see it."

16

COOPER

"She'll show up."

Cammi's said the same thing for the last three days and still, Lila hasn't shown her face at the shop. I don't know why I thought she would. She's pissed at me and this job wasn't real for her anyway.

"It doesn't matter," I say when I turn away from the new window.

"If it doesn't matter, why do you keep staring at the parking lot like you're trying to make her magically appear?"

I'm saved from answering when the alarm beeps and a customer walks through the front door. Not only did I have all the damage fixed, but I also had a new security system installed. Fifty-five hundred dollars and every penny is a penny well spent.

"Morning." I greet the customer. "Do you have an appointment?"

"No," the man replies, his gaze darting everywhere but at me. "I was hoping you'd have time for a walk-in."

I watch for a moment as he fidgets with his hands and continues to avoid looking at me. There's something about him that seems *off,* but I chalk it up to first-time jitters, especially since I see no visible tattoos.

I glance at the clock on the wall. "I've got a client coming in soon, but I've got another artist who's free right now. Any thoughts on what you want?"

He finally looks at me. "Are you Cooper?"

It's an innocent enough question but with everything going on, it makes me wary and my defensive instincts kick in. "Who's asking?"

"Name's Shawn," he replies, his tone even. "A friend of mine recommended you. Said you're the best in the business, at least in this town." He waves a hand in a dismissive gesture. "I wanted to be sure of who you were since it's you who I want to do that ink."

My defensiveness eases a bit. I know I have reason to be leery, but I remind myself that I can't take it out on clients.

"Right. Sorry."

"Hey, man, no problem. I drove by the other day and noticed the vandalism to your shop, so your cautiousness is to be expected."

"Appreciate the understanding." I smile at a woman who walks through the door. "If you wanna stick around, I can squeeze you in after my appointment, depending on the size of what you want."

"Nah, that's okay." Shawn extends his hand and I shake it. "I'll stop by another time."

Before I even have a chance to offer to schedule him an appointment, he's gone. The whole exchange was weird, but I don't have time to analyze it. I've got work to do.

Cammi checks in my appointment, a college girl who wants her sorority letters tattooed on the top of her foot. I prep my station and when all the paperwork is completed, she settles into the chair.

"That tickles." She giggles when the first press of the needle hits her skin.

No, it doesn't tickle. It's a fucking needle.

College Girl talks through the entire process. Incessant, nonstop words about whatever it is that sorority girls find important.

"So, what do ya say?"

"About?" I ask.

I lift the tattoo gun away from her foot. I'm finished and want to get through the aftercare instructions and get her out of here. She's on my last nerve.

"The party tonight," she replies. "Wanna come?"

"No."

Her face falls and I know I should apologize for being short with her, but I can't bring myself to do it. I review the pamphlet of instructions with her and when I go to put on the wrap, she refuses, saying something about wanting to be sure people see it right away.

She's being ridiculous. Her jeans are long enough that they cover the ink anyway but no matter what I tell her, she doesn't budge. I warn her of the consequences one last time and then, thankfully, Cammi appears.

"Why don't you come with me and I'll get you checked out?"

College Girl spares me one last glance and as she's heading toward the front counter, she calls over her shoulder. "Your loss."

"Don't fucking care," I mumble under my breath.

I focus on cleaning up and sanitizing everything so it's ready for the next client. I hear the chirp of the alarm and breathe a sigh of relief that the girl is gone, only to have that illusion shattered by Cammi's words.

"Hey, Lila! I told him you'd show."

Motherfucker!

"Yeah. Sorry about the last few days. I haven't been feeling great."

Bullshit. She's been avoiding me.

I try to tune out the rest of their conversation but find it impossible. Especially when I hear her next few words.

"You remember Nate, right?"

I whirl around and that's when I realize that Lila didn't come in alone. My vision gets hazy and my entire body burns as if someone is pumping lava straight into my veins through an IV.

"Yeah," Cammi responds. She must sense a shift in me because she looks right at me before returning her attention to Lila and Nate. "Uh, Nate, what brings you here today? Are you wanting a tattoo?"

Cammi's tone sounds hopeful, like she knows that I'm dangerously close to losing my shit if she doesn't intervene.

"Nah. Just hanging out with Lila."

Cammi can't stop looking back and forth between me and them and Nate eventually follows her gaze.

"Dude, what's your problem?" he asks with a level of disrespect that would get him shot in some places.

Lila is the last one to look in my direction and when she does, her expression morphs from one of casual indifference to one of defiant stubbornness. My blood boils.

"Dude?" I stalk toward them and while Lila stands her ground, Nate backs up a step. "I'm not your *'dude'*. I am, however, her boss." I point to Lila. "And she's on the clock, so I suggest you get the fuck out."

"And if I refuse?" Nate counters.

I grab the little shit by his collar and yank him toward me. "You don't fucking want to know," I reply with steel in my voice.

The voice in my head is screaming at me to stop, to get over it and let Lila have her fun. After all, I was the one that pushed her away. And as much as I know it's wrong, not my place, I don't want her to be with anyone else.

Nate yanks out of my hold and smooths his hands down his shirt. "Fine, man." He turns to face Lila. "Call me later if you need a ride home. I'm outta here."

He storms out of the shop and I'm left standing there like an idiot. Lila and Cammi are both staring daggers at me, no doubt plotting my murder. I don't acknowledge either of them while I force air in and out of my lungs, my chest heaving as if I just ran a marathon.

I'm so caught up in trying to calm down that I don't see Lila take a step toward me. I don't register the hand flying at me until her palm connects with my cheek in a stinging slap.

"Don't you *ever* do that again," she seethes.

With wide eyes, I stare at her, shocked speechless that she actually struck me.

"Really, now you don't speak?" she shouts. "What the hell is your problem?"

"Guys, why don't you—"

I hold a hand up to silence Cammi but don't take my eyes off Lila. "You wanna know what my problem is?"

She crosses her arms over her chest, pushing her cleavage up and making it almost impossible to focus. I manage though.

"You, Sprite. My problem is you."

"Fuck you, Cooper."

Lila turns on her heel and rushes out the front door. I watch as she pulls her cell phone out of her back pocket and places a call, presumably to get a ride.

"Dammit, Cooper," Cammi admonishes as she stomps toward me. "Why are you pushing her away? You like her. I can see it every time you two are in the same room. What is the matter with you?"

"It doesn't matter."

"Yeah, it does matter. I get that you're stressed out right now with everything that's going on but don't let the shitstorm take over your life." Cammi loosens her stance and wraps her arms around me in a hug. "You deserve to be happy, Cooper. More so than anyone I know."

"I've got responsibilities. Happy can wait."

"I'm not sure if you're aware but you can handle responsibilities and be happy at the same time. It is possible. People all over the world do it every single day."

I look down at her and see the smirk on her face. Cammi has always had the ability to be completely serious and teasing at the same time.

"I'll make you a deal," she offers. I arch a brow in question. "If you really don't like Lila, fine, I'll back off. I'll let you be a miserable ass and never bring it up again. But," she pauses, and all the teasing is gone. "If you like her and there's something else holding you back, then talk to her. Tell her how you feel and see how it plays out."

"She's your best friend, Cam." The argument is weak, even to my ears, but it doesn't mean it's any less valid.

"So? That's even better in my book." Her smile widens and the dimples she's had since she was a baby pop out. "You and Lila are two of my favorite people in the world. If being together makes you happy, then I'm all for it."

"I killed someone."

"You saved your sisters," Cammi counters.

I lock eyes with her, searching for something, anything that would validate my fears but all I find is love and understanding and acceptance.

"You make it sound so simple."

"And you're making it harder than it has to be."

Cammi breaks eye contact and looks out the front window. I follow her gaze and see Lila sitting on the curb. I have no idea what she's thinking or feeling but her back is hunched like she has her knees drawn up to her chest.

"It's your move, big brother."

17

LILA

*I*diot.
         Immature.
Stupid.

Those are the words that are going through my mind, over and over again like a never-ending movie reel. I knew that showing up at the shop with Nate would set Cooper off and I did it anyway. I don't think that's what my mom had in mind when she told me to make Cooper see that he's good enough for me.

So fucking stupid.

I tried calling Nate to come back and get me, but he didn't answer. So here I am, sulking on the curb, praying the sky will open up and suck me into the abyss.

A beep alerts me that someone is leaving the shop and I assume it's Cammi coming to talk me into going back inside.

"I'm not going in there. Not as long as he's—"

I slam my mouth shut when Cooper sits next to me and stretches his legs out in front of him. His shoulder brushes up against mine and I hate the involuntary reaction his touch elicits. Even when I hate him, I want him.

"What do you want?"

"Would you believe me if I told you I want to apologize?"

There's a hopeful quality in the way he asks that pulls a smile from me. "Oh yeah? For what?"

"I think it'd be easier to list what the apology *isn't* for," he says with a self-deprecating chuckle.

"I'm listening."

Cooper pulls his legs in and wraps his arms around his knees. He stares off into the distance and is quiet for so long, I start to wonder if he's going to actually apologize or if he's having second thoughts. Second thoughts seem to be something he's comfortable with so it wouldn't surprise me.

Finally, he opens his mouth and I brace myself for what's about to come out but what does is the last thing I expect.

"Will you have dinner with me tonight?"

I almost swallow my damn tongue. He wouldn't have shocked me any more if he had said that Santa Claus and the Easter Bunny are real. I sit up straight and force myself to not jump up like a giddy little kid.

"Um, like a date?"

"I'm thinking more like a meal between friends."

My shoulders sag. "Oh. So Carmen and Cammi will be there?"

His gaze cuts to me. "What? No."

I bite the inside of my cheek to keep from seeming too excited. He can say it's not a date but if we're alone, there's still hope.

"Okay."

His forehead wrinkles and he studies me as if searching for answers to questions that he doesn't even know. I resist the urge to reach out and smooth the creases away.

"Seriously?" he asks.

I shrug. "Sure. Why not?"

Cooper gets to his feet and runs his fingers through his

hair. "Great. Perfect. That's…" He shakes his head and starts to walk backward toward the door. "I'll just go get Cammi so she can take you home. Unless you wanna stay and work?"

I push up from the curb and brush the dust and dirt off my ass. "I can stay."

We both go inside, and Cooper's demeanor immediately shifts from nervous man to confident business owner and boss so fast my head spins. I join Cammi at the front desk and she practically vibrates with curiosity.

I decide to put her out of her misery. "We're having dinner tonight."

She squeals with excitement and I slap a hand over her mouth and dart my eyes toward Cooper's office, where he disappeared to. When she stills, I pull my hand back.

"Sorry," she says. "But that's great."

"He says it's not a date."

"Do you want it to be?"

"Yes," I say, without hesitation.

"Then I say treat it like one." Her smile is so big that I can't help but think that it's gotta hurt her cheeks. "I've got an idea. Be right back."

She rushes into Cooper's office, not bothering to knock, and leaves the door open. I can hear them talking but can't make out the words. When she comes back, she's even giddier than before.

"Let's go."

Cammi grabs my hand and practically drags me out the door and to the car.

"Where are we going?"

"We are going to prep for your date." She spares me a glance before turning out of the parking lot in the direction of our favorite places to shop. "I'm thinking manicure, pedicure, hair, new outfit… the works."

Her excitement is contagious and before I know it, the

radio is cranked up and we're belting out the lyrics to "Wrecking Ball" like we're Miley Cyrus herself. It doesn't take long to arrive at our destination and when we get there, a thought occurs to me.

"Cam, are you sure it's a good idea to do this?" At her questioning look, I continue. "I mean, with everything going on, I'm surprised Cooper is okay with this."

"What my brother doesn't know won't kill him." She winks.

Normally, I wouldn't give lying a second thought, but I can't shake the feeling that this is a bad idea. I've given it a lot of thought and while I really don't think I'm in any danger—I'm not the Knights of Wrath's enemy—Cammi is.

Cammi apparently picks up on my unease and tries to reassure me. "We'll be fine, Lila. I promise. No one even knows we're here."

I let myself relax and force my worries aside. "Okay."

As we walk toward the salon entrance, I can't help but pay extra attention to our surroundings. Nothing seems out of place but I'm not sure I'd even notice if it did. The salon isn't a regular destination of ours.

"Ladies, welcome."

We're greeted by a young, friendly woman who takes the time to find out what we want. The mani/pedi is first and we soak up the pampering like a sponge soaks up water. When it's time to have my hair done, I tell the guy I just want a trim but Cammi is having none of that.

"C'mon, girl. Go big. Be bold."

I stare at my reflection in the mirror and assess my current hair situation. I've always had blonde hair and never contemplated anything different. My eyes meet the hairdresser's in the glass, and he tilts his head as if examining me.

"May I make a suggestion?" he asks.

"Sure."

He takes a few moments to fluff up my hair and then pulls it straight by the ends. It's like he's an artist and has to inspect the canvas before he can start creating.

"You've got great bone structure and incredible hair, so I don't want to change too much. Just, glam it up a little. I'm thinking platinum, almost silver, color with layers to add texture. A soft, wavy curl to top it off."

I try to envision what he's describing and the image that I have in my head is one I love.

"Go for it."

Four hours later I'm walking outside feeling like a million bucks. The guy was right, the new hairstyle adds a bit of glam but isn't so much that I lose that edgy vibe I've always gone for. My nails are matte black and only add to the overall image.

"Cooper is gonna shit when he sees you." She slings her arm around my shoulder as we walk to the car. "No way will he even remember all the reasons you're off-limits."

I stop in my tracks and pull away to look at her. "What?"

Cammi's excitement disappears and her eyes are wide. "Shit. Forget I said anything."

"No, Cam, I won't forget it. What do you mean he thinks I'm off-limits?"

She chews on a freshly manicured nail and looks everywhere but at me.

"Cammi?" I prod.

She flings her arm down and huffs out a breath. "It's nothing. He just…"

"He just what?"

"He can't let go of the past, of what he did. Add to it that you're my best friend and he's doing everything he can to keep you at arm's length."

"That's ridiculous."

"That's what I said." The words come out of her in a rush.

"I told him that I don't care if you two get together and that he should just talk to you about things instead of sabotaging it."

"And that's why he asked me to dinner."

All of a sudden, things start to fall into place. The way he kissed me and then tried to apologize. The way he sucks me into his orbit and then pushes me away. The way he does everything he can to back me up when it comes to my family but then treats me like a child.

It all makes sense. The puzzle pieces that have been missing are in the palm of my hand and I just have to lock them into place. My mom was right. I have to show him, make him see me, see the potential, see *us*.

I know exactly what I need to do. I grab Cammi's hand and drag her the rest of the way to the car.

"We've got some shopping to do."

18

COOPER

Forty-two minutes.
  That's how long I have to get ready for my date with Lila.

Not a date. That's what you told her. Dinner between friends. Nothing more.

I strip my clothes off and toss them on the bathroom floor before stepping under the hot spray. The water seeps into my muscles but the tension doesn't ease. I'm nervous as hell and I can't tell if it's because I haven't been out with a woman in a long time or if it's because, after tonight, if all goes as planned, I'll have no more secrets.

I was distracted at work trying to figure out where this dinner should take place. I considered a restaurant but dismissed that idea pretty quickly. The things I have to say don't need to be said in public. Besides, it's not safe. I have no idea who is a threat and it's not worth risking it. Lila would be safe if it weren't for me and I refuse to intentionally put her in the crosshairs.

The only thing I managed to do after Cammi and Lila left the shop was to piss off my staff and stress myself out with every single scenario for tonight playing out in my head. Oh, and text Lila to tell her to come here at seven. I still have no idea where we'll go and I'm guessing that now I only have roughly thirty-four minutes to figure it out.

I shut off the water and reach out to grab a towel and wrap it around my waist. I spend a few minutes trimming my beard and can't help but wish we were back in our own house. I don't have an actual bedroom here since I let the girls have them, so I have to finish getting ready in the steamy haze from my shower.

Not to mention, no bedroom equals no sex.

I ignore the voice in my head. Tonight isn't about sex, although I can't deny that I crave it. Hell, after I say what I have to say, Lila may tell me and my dick to fuck off.

A knock at the door startles me and I topple over as I'm pulling my jeans up. I manage to stay upright and get them buttoned.

"What?" I call out.

"She's gonna be here any minute," Cammi calls through the door.

I pick up my cell from the counter and tap the screen to bring up the time. Shit! Four minutes left. I slip my shirt on, spray some cologne, and call it good.

"Where are you taking her?" Cammi asks the second I open the door.

I urge her to the side and walk past her. "No fucking clue."

"Coop," she cries. "How is that even possible? You've had all day to figure this out."

"I know," I snap, my nerves getting the better of me.

"You better figure it out quick."

I glare at her. "Don't you have somewhere to be?"

Cammi agreed to take Carmen to the main house while I'm gone. They're safe enough on BRB property but the last thing I need is to worry about them while I'm with Lila. I talked with Isaiah and he said it was fine for them to come and hang out.

Cammi huffs out a breath. "Fine. We're leaving." She turns on her heel and knocks on Carmen's door. "Time to go."

Within two minutes, they're both gone, and I'm left to pace while I wait. The seconds tick by and the longer I wait, the more nervous I become. By the time twenty-five minutes pass, I'm past the nerves and anger begins to settle in.

Where the hell is she?

I check my cell to see if I missed a call or text but there's nothing. I compose a quick text asking her where she is and just as I hit send, I hear footsteps on the porch. I throw open the door, prepared to lay into her, but as soon as I see her, my brain turns to mush and my anger fades.

Lila looks from her phone to me. "I'm right here."

Incapable of speech, or any coherent thought for that matter, I let my eyes roam over her. She's not the same person she was this morning, not by a long shot. Gone is the nineteen-year-old college co-ed and in her place stands the most stunning representation of beauty I've ever seen. Her jeans hug her body perfectly and the rips expose little teases of flesh. The red top is form-fitting and the way it accentuates her curves has me itching to touch her.

Lila glances down at herself and when she lifts her eyes to mine, her face falls. "You don't like it."

"I…"

When she starts to turn around, I reach out and grip her arm to yank her toward me. Her chest slams into mine and I press my lips to hers. I thread my fingers through her hair, and she digs her nails into my chest. I slant my mouth and press my tongue past the seam to tangle it with hers.

I don't want the kiss to end and judging by the way I'm having to swallow her moans, neither does she. But I know I have to, especially if I want to have anything resembling a conversation with her.

I break away from her and step back. Her eyes remain closed for a moment and when they flutter open, there's a fire in them.

"You're so fucking sexy," I growl. "You already were but now..." My gaze travels the length of her body again. "Now you're insanely gorgeous."

A grin spreads across her face and color flags her cheeks.

"Thanks. You're not so bad yourself."

I chuckle at her words and she does the same. The air crackles around us but I have a feeling that's not likely to change any time soon. Not with her looking like she does, not with her looking *at me* like she is.

"So, where are we going?"

"Honestly, I don't know."

"I have an idea." A devilish grin appears. "Do you trust me?"

"I don't like the sound of that."

"Just answer the question. Do you trust me?"

"Yes."

"Good." She glances toward the side of the cabin. "Cammi told me you went back to your place and got your bike."

I narrow my eyes at her. "I did."

"Feel like riding?"

I love to ride and the thought of her with her arms around my waist and thighs pressing against mine from the back of my Harley sends my libido into overdrive.

"Always."

I turn to head toward my bike, expecting her to follow, but when I realize she's not right beside me, I glance over my shoulder and see her standing in the same spot.

"You coming?"

"Meet me at my parent's place."

Before I can ask why, she turns and starts jogging away. I watch her for a minute or two, dumbfounded. What the hell is she doing? When she's out of sight, I give in and fire up my bike.

Other than bringing it here, I haven't ridden in a while. Since I have no idea what she's got up her sleeve, I double-check all the gauges making sure that I've got enough gas for whatever it might be. I also make sure that there are two helmets in the saddlebags. Satisfied that I'm as ready as I can be, I take off to meet her.

When I pull up in front of her place, I'm shocked to see her straddling a black Harley with yellow detailing. She looks comfortable, like she belongs there.

"Whose bike is that?" I ask when I pull up beside her.

"Mine."

"Huh."

"My parents got it for me for my sixteenth birthday. It didn't always look this good, but I had money saved up and then used what I got for high school graduation to get the custom paint job done."

"I'm impressed."

"Thanks." She revs the idling engine. "Follow me."

Lila takes off leaving me with no other choice than to do just that. She leads me away from the familiar and we head down curvy back roads. I have no idea where we're going or if she even has a destination in mind, but I don't give a damn. Watching her handle the beast beneath her stirs something in me that's been gone for a long time. Something I hardly recognize.

We reach a straight stretch of road and Lila takes off like a shot and I swear I can hear her laughing over the wind whipping around me.

Happy. For the first time in a long time, way too long to even quantify, I'm happy.

19

LILA

"That was incredible."

I shake out my hair after hanging my helmet on the handlebar. I have no doubt that my locks are a mess, but it doesn't matter. Cooper let go for the first time ever, that I've seen, so it's worth it.

"Riding has always, I don't know, centered me."

"You continue to surprise me, Sprite."

My face flushes at the nickname. The first time he called me that, I was annoyed, frustrated because I thought he was making fun of me but now? I like it. It feels more like a flirty tease than a put-down.

Cooper clears his throat. "I don't know about you but I'm starving."

"Me too. And if I remember right, you said this was supposed to be dinner."

"I did." He heaves a sigh. "But I never did figure out the details."

"Then I guess you're just gonna have to keep trusting me."

Without thinking, I link my fingers with his and start walking toward the main house. At first, he's stiff. He's holding my hand without really holding it. After a few minutes, his grip tightens, and my heart skips a beat.

At the main house, we're greeted by raucous laughter and what appears to be a pool tournament going on. Everyone is so caught up in the competition and trash-talking that we manage to slip past them into the kitchen.

Cooper follows my lead, and we make a few sandwiches. I throw them into a cloth grocery bag, along with a Ziploc baggie filled with Oreos and another filled with potato chips. Cooper snags a few drinks out of the fridge and adds them to the bag.

"I think we've got everything we need. Let's go."

We manage to slip back out without being spotted and I snag a blanket off the couch on our way through the living room. I lead him toward the field where we used to hang out when we were teenagers. It's nothing special but it is secluded and also on the property, so it's safe.

Cooper takes the blanket from me and spreads it out. I kick off my boots, yank my socks off, and sit down to slide my toes through the grass. He laughs at me but then does the same.

"Is this your version of a make-out spot?" I lean back and brace myself on my palms. "Are you trying to seduce me, Sprite?"

I throw my head back on a laugh. "As if that would work."

"The thing is, it would."

My gaze snaps to him, questions dancing around in my head, ones that I don't know how to put into words.

"I like you, Lila." Cooper leans back and mirrors my pose. He tips his head back and stares at the darkening sky. "More than I have any right to."

"What makes you so sure of that? That you don't have a right to like me, I mean?"

He doesn't answer me right away and I begin to think he never will but then he opens his mouth.

"You know I killed my dad. You know where I come from." The silhouette of his face shows a tortured soul, one as damaged and broken as I imagine is possible. "Fuck, you were attacked because of who I am. Add in the fact that you're my *little* sister's best friend, and we're doomed before we even start."

His emphasis on the word 'little' triggers my temper but I keep it in check. He asked me to dinner for a reason and I'm guessing it's because he wants to talk. Fine. I'll let him talk. And then he's gonna listen.

I say nothing and sit up straight to get the food out. He remains where he is and appears to not even be paying attention. My sandwich is almost gone when he starts talking again.

"There's something you need to know about me."

"What's that?" I ask when he doesn't elaborate.

Cooper's Adam's apple bobs when he swallows. "When I killed my father, I loved every second of it." Another swallow. "I watched the blood seep from his body and the life drain from his eyes and I didn't want to stop watching. I *couldn't* stop."

He sits up and props his forearms on his knees. While he stares off into the distance, I pop an Oreo in my mouth.

"I think, on some level, I always knew that I'd have to kill him. But I never thought I'd enjoy it. When Cammi called me that afternoon and I heard the chaos in the background, I knew it was the day. The only way his life wasn't ending that day was if mine did first."

My heart breaks for him and I swear I can feel the cracks spreading like tiny little spider veins.

"No matter how much shit he put us through, how much abuse we endured, that doesn't change the fact that I murdered him. It doesn't change what I'm capable of. I'd do it over and over again if I could. Hell, I *wish* I could. I would torture him in as many ways as I could think of, each one worse than the last."

Cooper's tone is violent, blood-thirsty, but he doesn't scare me. I want him to keep going, keep purging all the evil he thinks is in him.

"He lay dead next to my lifeless mother. He didn't deserve to be anywhere near her, even in death, but I couldn't do anything about it. I had two scared girls who were now dependent on me. They were locked in the bathroom, Cammi holding a gun and ready to pull the trigger if she had to. I couldn't grieve or scream or cry. There was no time for that. I had to get them out of the house all the while trying to keep them from seeing the devastation in the living room."

He pauses and scrubs his hands over his face. The only visible sign that this is hard for him is the lines on his face. The ones that make him seem far older than he really is. The ones I want to touch.

"Anyway, I got them out of there and we headed straight to the police station. I turned myself in. I was prepared though. I also handed over a flash drive that contained pictures documenting years of physical abuse. I have my mom to thank for that. When I turned sixteen, she gave it to me with instructions to turn it in when it was time." Cooper sighs and it almost resembles a chuckle. "I remember asking her how I would know it was time and ya know what she said?"

"What?"

"'Son, you'll know. I promise you'll know.'" He glances at me and his eyes are glassy. "She knew, Lila. Years before he killed her, she knew. Why the fuck didn't she leave? Why didn't she take us and run like hell? Why didn't she protect us? Protect me?"

A tear rolls down his cheek. While it matches his words, it's in stark contrast to the fury that's trembling through him. I brush it away with my thumb. He clenches and unclenches his hands and sucks in a few deep breaths.

"I was never charged with a crime. To this day, I'm not sure if it's because they really believed I was in actual danger that day and it was self-defense or if they saw the pictures on the flash drive and were just secretly glad that I rid the world of his filth."

Cooper stretches his legs out and grabs his sandwich.

"I don't really give a shit why. It doesn't matter. I may not have been behind bars, but we still couldn't have a funeral for our mom, we couldn't mourn or say goodbye. What I'd done brought the cops to the club's door. The club didn't care that that wasn't my intention. The cops went to our house to process the scene and came across a lot of stuff that implicated, at the very least, the senior members. They ended up doing some further investigation into the club and arrested most of them. I was a pariah and by extension, so were Cammi and Carmen. I'd committed the worst kind of betrayal. They didn't care about what was going on behind closed doors. All they cared about was the club's reputation and enterprises and I'd destroyed that. With one pull of the trigger, I ended one Hell and created another."

I mull over all of the information that Cooper's given me while he eats his food. He is so convinced that he's toxic because he came from toxic. What he doesn't see is he's anything and everything but. After the last chip is gone, Cooper leans back on his elbows and keeps talking.

"I never really gave the consequences of my actions much thought, at least as far as they pertain to me. I cared about one thing and one thing only: Cammi and Carmen's safety and happiness. As long as I got them away from there and provided them with as normal a life as possible, that's all that mattered. I didn't care about myself or whether or not I was happy. I have my sisters, my shop, my *life*. And that was always enough. I was okay with settling for *enough*."

Cooper rolls his neck and pins me with his stare.

"Until you."

20

COOPER

"Enough is *never* enough."

Lila's hair sways around her face as she gets to her feet and when her eyes lock on mine, they shimmer with emotion. She props her hands on her hips and glares at me. I push myself up off the ground and step toward her.

"I knew you'd hate—"

"Shut up!"

"Excuse me."

"I sat here quietly while you talked. I have no doubt that you thought I'd go running the second you stopped but guess what? I'm still fucking here and now you're gonna let me talk. You're gonna stand there and listen to every damn word I have to say."

I nod and mentally prepare myself for her to sling insults and hatred and anger. I brace for the worst because the worst is what I deserve.

"First of all—and this is perhaps one of the most important things you need to listen to—enough is never enough." She rises up on her tiptoes and places her hands on my cheeks. "Do you hear me? Enough. Is. Never. Enough."

"But—"

"No buts, Coop. Zero, zilch, nada." She lets her arms fall and her chest heaves. "Do you think that Carmen and Cammi should settle for anything less than everything?" I'm afraid to open my mouth so I don't. "Answer me, dammit. Do you?"

"Of course not."

"You say that their happiness and safety is all that matters to you. And that's great. That makes you who you are. The fact that you put others so far above yourself makes you an incredible man. But there comes a point where it also makes you incredibly stupid."

"What the—"

"Let me finish." She starts to pace and it's several minutes before she continues. "As much as you love your sisters, as much as you want nothing but good things for them… it goes both ways, Coop. How can they possibly be truly happy if you're not? You're their brother, the father they should have always had, their damn hero, all wrapped up into one amazing human. You may not see it and maybe you never will, but I do. Even before I knew the story, I could see how much they love you, how they worship you."

"They shouldn't."

"I'm not done," she snaps. "I get that you've got demons. I get that you carry so much trash in your head. I mean, who wouldn't? But you've gotta let it go." She stops pacing and looks at me, her expression begging me to hear her. "You should really talk to the original Brotherhood members. I think you'll be surprised by what you learn."

"I'll think about it."

"Okay. If you decide to, then ask them about their lives. About their existence before the club. About what they've gone through, how broken and lost they've been. And then they'll tell you that, yes, it changed them, in ways they couldn't have imagined, but it made them stronger, better. Fuck, Sadie and Brie's stories alone will give you chills. And let's not forget my mom. She had to watch her daughter be thrown off a bridge and there was nothing she could do to stop it." My eyes widen and I reach for her, but she steps away. "It wasn't me." She pauses to catch her breath. "Do you get what I'm saying here?"

"I think so."

"Cooper, demons aren't unique to you. We all have shit. Anyone who says otherwise is a damn fool. Anyway, will you do that for me? Will you talk to them? I think you'll learn a lot. I also think you'll find exactly what you need to heal, to move past, well, your past."

"And what is that?"

"Family."

That one word knocks the wind out of me, and I struggle to stay upright. Is it really that simple?

"Loyalty, acceptance, trust, strength, goodness, brotherhood... *love*." I lift my eyes to meet hers. "You'll find all of that, too."

The corners of my mouth tip up. "How did you get so wise?"

Lila glares at me but I can tell she's fighting off a grin. "I've been trying to tell everyone, I'm not a damn child."

"No, Sprite, you're not."

"I know I'm young, Coop. But age is just a number. Hey, at least I'm not jailbait." She laughs at herself but quickly sobers. "I was raised knowing all about the evil in the world. I was shielded from it, put in a bubble so it wouldn't touch me. But it's always been there and no matter how hard we try, no matter how many people like the BRB are in the world, it's always gonna be there. But you are not evil. You are not even remotely what I was protected from. Maybe some people would be scared, and I'll even go so far as to say most nineteen-year-olds are too immature to handle you or your past or your demons. I'm not one of those people, Coop."

"I'm beginning to see that."

"I can keep going if you need more convincing."

"Lila, I can't promise you that I'll never worry or that you won't have to remind me every once in a while about that age being just a number thing. I don't even know if I can promise to stick around if the Knights of Wrath keep coming for me. You have to know that." I cup her cheek and she leans into my palm. "You have to know that I won't risk Cammi or Carmen, I won't risk you. Not for anything."

"Can you at least promise that you won't leave without saying goodbye?"

"Yes."

"Can you promise not to shut me out?"

"Yes."

She reaches up and loosely wraps her arms around my neck.

"Can you promise to give us a chance? To see where this goes?"

"Yes."

Lila jumps up and I catch her easily. She locks her ankles at the small of my back and fuses her lips to mine. All of my worries immediately disappear, and I'm thrown into the hottest kiss of my life.

My hands slide up the back of her shirt and I find her skin bare. She moans as my fingertips trace over her flesh. With her body wrapped around mine, I lower us to the ground, never breaking the kiss.

Her arms fall to her sides, but they don't stay there long. Her hands clumsily work the button on my jeans and when she tugs the zipper down, my cock jumps. Lila doesn't make a move to free my rigid length but instead lifts her arms to rest them in the grass above her head.

I move my mouth from her lips to her chin and then trail them lower to nip at the pulse point in her neck. Her head thrashes from side to side and her moans grow louder.

Lila's responsiveness to my every move spurs me on. I'm straddling her hips and when I get my fill of the flesh at her throat, I slide down her legs and lift the hem of her shirt to expose her flat stomach. I pepper kisses around her belly button and work my way up and use my teeth to tug the fabric over her perfect tits.

I circle one nipple with my tongue while I pinch the other between my fingers and roll it.

"Gah, Coop," Lila groans.

Lila squirms beneath me and I'm so hard I'm afraid my dick will shatter if any pressure is applied. She reaches for my shirt and attempts to pull it over my head and when she can't get it, I yank it off myself. Cool air washes over my skin but it does nothing to tamper the raging fire threatening to burn me up.

Unable to hold back, I strip her bare and make quick work of taking the rest of my own clothes off. Lila's hands move to cover her pussy and hide herself from me.

"Don't," I command as I wrap my fingers around her wrists and pin her arms to her sides. "I need to see you, all of you."

Suddenly, the bold and sassy Lila that I've come to know disappears and is replaced by a shy, almost awkward version. She struggles to maintain eye contact and when she finally does, she squeezes those pretty green orbs shut.

Warning bells go off in my head. "Lila, what's wrong?" When she doesn't respond, I lean down and place a kiss on one eye and then the other. "Lila, talk to me."

"I..." She takes a deep breath and holds it for a second before puffing her cheeks out and releasing the air. "I just..."

A thought occurs to me. "Lila, baby, are you a virgin?"

Her eyes open wide and she shakes her head. "No! No, I'm not. I'm just not... I've only ever been with Drake. And it wasn't... I'm not... I want this to be good for you but what if I screw it up?"

She looks so adorably panicked and it only endears me to her more than I already am. While I'm not shocked that she's more inexperienced than she's let on, I'm glad I asked because now I know I need to slow things down and focus on her.

"Aw, Sprite, there is nothing you could do to screw it up. Not a damn thing."

"What if—"

I capture her lips with mine to stop whatever nonsense is about to come out of her mouth. I kiss her until she's squirming and then pull away slightly so I can see her face.

"Not. A. Damn. Thing."

She nods but her agreement isn't convincing.

"We're gonna take things slow, okay?" Another nod. As I'm talking, I reach between us and lazily circle her clit with my finger. "If there's something you like, let me know." Her lips part and her hips buck. "And if there's something you don't like, tell me that, too."

I increase the pressure and watch as her face relaxes. I glide my finger through her folds and coat it with her natural lubricant. I thrust one finger inside her, slowly at first. Paying attention to her facial expressions and how she responds to my movements, I add a second finger and use my thumb to stimulate her clit.

"You like that, Sprite?"

"Mmm."

I alternate between finger fucking her and giving her

most sensitive bundle of nerves the attention it's throbbing for. I don't let up until her moans grow louder and her walls clamp down as she flies over the edge.

"That's it, baby. Let it happen."

Her orgasm is the best aphrodisiac and I know once my cock is inside her, my own will be explosive. When her body stills, I simply stare at her, take in the most beautiful sight I've ever seen.

"That was so good," she mumbles drowsily.

"Ah, Sprite, we're not done."

Always paying attention to her, I grip my length and line it up with her wet pussy. Her eyes lock on mine when I push the tip past her plump flesh. When her nostrils flare, I ease all the way in and hold still for a moment so I don't make a fool of myself.

As hard as it is to keep myself from losing it immediately, I manage. I pull out and thrust back in. My arms are trembling from holding my weight off of her, but I don't lower myself. I don't want to lose sight of her face, not for a moment.

After several thrusts, her hips start to move, and I increase the pace. In, out, in, out. Long, smooth strokes that are driving me insane with need. Tingles race up and down my spine and I know I'm close. Too close.

I brace myself on one arm and drag my free hand down her torso to her clit. Without slowing my thrusts, I rub fast circles on the little nub. That combination is all it takes, and she cries out her release.

The spasms of her climax drag me over the cliff with her. I can't stop the fireworks from dancing in my vision and our shouts seem to echo around us. My arms give out and I collapse but I'm able to roll to the side so I don't crush her.

I turn my head so I can see Lila's face and the satisfied smile I see causes my heart to feel like it's going to burst.

"Like I said, you could never screw it up."

We both chuckle and I can't help but fall a little more for this amazing woman. She's everything I don't deserve and everything I've always wanted, wrapped up in a perfect little package.

Lila curls into my side and sighs in contentment. Part of me wishes we weren't in a field, that we were back at my place, in my bed. But the rest of me, the sated part of me, recognizes that where we are is perfect.

"Cooper?"

I tuck my chin and look down at her. "Yeah?"

"I'm glad you asked me to dinner."

I smile against her hair. "Me too, Sprite."

She kicks her leg over mine. Her breathing starts to even out and I know she's close to sleep.

"Cooper?"

"Yeah?"

"I'm really sorry about your mom."

I'm silent for a few minutes but I hold Lila a little tighter. When her breathing evens out again and I'm sure she's asleep, I release a long sigh.

"Me too, Sprite. Me, too."

21

LILA

"I swear to God, Sprite, you've gotta start coming to work in baggy sweats or something."

I rest my palms on Cooper's chest. I'm sitting on the edge of his desk and he's standing between my thighs. His thick length is straining against his jeans and I'm loving every second of it.

"Or what?" I taunt him.

He growls at me and leans in to nip at my bottom lip. I pull away but don't make it far before he tugs me toward him and latches onto my earlobe. My panties are damp, and I want nothing more than for him to do wicked things to me.

"Fuck me, Coop," I say on a breathless moan.

I reach for his jeans and he grabs my wrists, holding them still. He straightens away from me and grins. I do not smile back. I want him and I want him now. I don't care that we're at work. There's a lock on his office door and contrary to my actions otherwise, I can be quiet.

"Do you have any idea what you're even asking for?"

I narrow my eyes at him. Of course, I know. I want his

cock inside me. What's not to understand? I give him a saucy grin.

"Yep."

"Sprite, I'm gonna let you in on a little secret."

I squirm, expecting something sexy to come out of his mouth before he gives in and has his way with me.

"And before you get all worked up, know that it has nothing to do with your age." Okay, not what I was hoping for. "You don't have the slightest clue what you're asking for. You've already told me that you've only been with Douchebag and I guarantee what he did wasn't fucking. You tell a man to fuck you... you tell *me* to fuck you, and I'm gonna fuck you. And I promise you, it'll be more than you bargain for and you'll love every single second."

A shiver races down my spine. If his plan is to scare me into backing off, he's failing miserably.

"Okay."

I reach for his waistband and he stops me... again.

"You're not listening."

"I heard every wo—"

"C'mon."

He lifts me off the desk and practically drags me from his office, through the shop, and out the door. He doesn't even pause when Beth and Corbin ask where we're going. To my surprise, he marches me down the sidewalk and through the entrance of Sandy's Lingerie and Gifts, the only other store in the strip mall.

Just inside, he comes to a halt and looks around. Heat infuses my body and suddenly I feel like I'm in a sauna. I'm sweating, my hands are shaking, I feel like I'm going to throw up.

"You've proved your point, Coop."

"What point would that be?"

"That I'm not experienced in the sack and I need to grow up."

"No, Sprite, that's not my point."

I fold my arms and tap my foot, anger starting to mix with embarrassment. "Then what is it?"

"My point is this: I want you. All the time, I want you. But yes, you are inexperienced." He holds his hand over my mouth when I try to interrupt. "And there is absolutely nothing wrong with that. Nothing. Do you hear me?" I nod because his hand is still pressing against my mouth. "I love that you've trusted me to teach you and help you discover what you want and what you like. I love making it exactly what you need. Slow and intimate with you is amazing."

"But?" I ask, although it's muffled behind his fingers.

He drops his hand and leans in to whisper, "But, you keep telling me to fuck you and there's gonna be nothing slow about it. Are you ready for that?"

When he takes a step back and waits for my answer, I glance around the store. Racks of lingerie fill the room but there's a doorway leading to another room and a sign that reads XXX above it. It's as if there's this forbidden portal to a hidden world. I think about what he's trying to tell me and realize that, while he's right and I didn't really know what I was asking, I'm intrigued and want to know.

"Are you ready for that?" he asks again.

"I…" My throat is dry, and I have to swallow several times before I can force words past my lips. "Yes, I'm ready for that."

He opens his mouth to respond but before he can get anything out, a woman steps through the XXX portal with a huge smile.

"Cooper!" she exclaims. "What brings you in today? There wasn't more vandalism, was there?"

"No, Patti, nothing like that."

"That's good to hear." Patti looks from Cooper to me and back again. "So, are you going to introduce us or let the poor girl stand there and wonder who the hell I am?"

"Woman," I retort without thinking.

"Patti, this is Lila." Cooper grins. "And as she so aptly put it, she's the *woman* I'm dating."

"It's about time." I turn toward another woman who seems to have appeared out of nowhere. "We've been wondering when you'd start to live a little."

"Hey, Wendy." Cooper leans to the side to glance past them. "Are the other ladies here? I'm sure they'll want to add their two cents."

I can hear the teasing in Cooper's tone, and I start to relax. If he's comfortable here, I can be too.

"They're all in the back, restocking some customer favorites." Patti winks. "So, is there something we can help you with, or do you two just want to browse and see what tickles your fancy?" She laughs at her own joke.

"Maybe a little of both. We'll look around for a bit but I'm sure she'll have some questions. Or maybe I will. Who knows?"

"Okay. We'll leave you be then."

Patti and Wendy disappear into the back room and Cooper turns to face me.

"I'm not gonna ask them any questions," I whisper fiercely.

"Trust me, you will."

"How do you know?"

"Because I'm not going to be able to answer them all. Some things you're just gonna need a woman's opinion on."

"This is stupid," I huff out.

"Do you trust me?"

"Of course I trust you."

"Good."

Cooper urges me through to the backroom and my eyes widen at everything lining the shelves and the displays. I look around and try to take it all in. I know what some of it is, just based on common sense, but there's a lot that I have no clue about. My gaze lands on what appears to be a kiddie pool.

"What the hell is a child's pool doing in a place like this?" I ask, genuinely confused.

"Oh, honey, that's a wrestling pool." My eyes shift to the left and I find yet another woman. "Sorry, I'm not trying to be nosy. But that," she points to the item in question. "That glorious thing provides the user with a place to get all down and dirty in the nude. Think of it as the X-rated version of mud wrestling but instead of mud, it comes with a five-gallon bucket of lube."

"Oh."

"I'm Tammie, by the way."

I shake her offered hand and find myself smiling and buzzing with excitement. What else will I find here? I walk around the perimeter of the room and peruse the shelves. There are movies, books, dildos, vibrators, edible panties, handcuffs, whips, and so much more. There's also a sex swing and I have to admit, it looks tempting as hell.

I realize that I have no clue if Cooper likes any of this stuff, but I have to assume he does if he brought me here. I double back to the far wall and spend what feels like a long time looking at the vibrators. I've never used one. I remember finding Tillie's in her nightstand several years ago, before Isaiah came back, and I wanted to know what it felt like but would never have used hers.

Cooper stands next to me and I can feel his eyes boring a hole into the top of my head.

"I want one."

Cooper chuckles. "Which one?"

I shrug. "You pick."

"Nope. This is one of those things you're gonna want their opinion on."

I glance around him but don't see any of the women. I decide to put the vibrators in the back of my mind and move on to something else. I return to the display case that holds the bondage stuff. My eyes land on the handcuffs and my breath hitches. Suddenly, I can't suck air into my lungs and panic hits me.

"Lila?"

Cooper's worried voice seeps through the fog and grounds me somehow. He lifts my chin and smiles.

"I will never hurt you. I will never do anything that makes you uncomfortable or scared."

My eyes slide closed.

"Look at me," he demands, and my lids flutter open. "See these hands?" He raises them and wiggles his fingers in front of my face. I nod. "These hands will only ever bring you pleasure. Never pain."

I nod again and force myself to regulate my breathing. "Okay."

"You good?"

"I'm good," I assure him.

"Now, do you see anything in there you want to try?"

"Do you like that stuff?"

"I can take it or leave it."

I return my attention to the display. There's a silk tie that catches my eye and a red feather that's tempting me. I point them out to Cooper and a devilish grin spreads.

"I can definitely take those."

"You two doing okay?"

Yet another woman enters the room. How many people work here?

"Hi, Lisa. We're good but Lila has a question about the

vibrators."

I elbow Cooper in the stomach for putting me on the spot.

"Sure thing." Lisa makes her way around the counter and stands in front of the large display. "Which one are you wondering about, hon?"

"That one." I point to what I think is a medium-sized pink one.

"Have you ever used a vibrator?" I shake my head. "Okay, then I'd recommend something else. That one isn't going to offer much as far as variation of the speed and vibration. Here," Lisa bends down and pulls one off a lower shelf. "This is what you need."

She hands the box to me. This one is much smaller and shaped almost like an egg. The Rabbit, as the box says, offers eleven different vibration settings and even boasts a remote control. I have no idea why it would need a remote or why I would want that many settings but if she recommends it, I'll give it a shot.

"I'll take it."

"Perfect. You're gonna love it." Lisa winks at me and sets the box by the register. "Cooper, make sure you check out the remote. Makes for some great foreplay."

"I'll definitely do that."

"So, anything else?"

"Yeah," Cooper responds. He hitches a thumb over his shoulder. "We'll take one of the silk ties and the red feather. Oh, and a bottle of the same lube I got last time. I don't remember the name."

"You got it."

Lisa disappears again to get the things Cooper asked for.

"So, use a lot of lube, do ya?" I try to cover up the fact that I'm jealous as hell, but he sees right through me.

"Sprite, I used the damn bottle all by myself." He lowers

his voice. "You're the first person I've been with since we left Nevada."

That fact shocks me and thrills me at the same time.

"Maybe I'll be your last."

Before he can respond, Lisa returns with her hands full. She gives us the items Cooper asked for, along with a receipt from the register.

"Take this all to the front and Sandy will ring you up."

"Thanks, Lisa."

"It's my pleasure, you know that." Cooper laughs and Lisa shifts her attention to me. "Honey, make this man buy you some lingerie next time you come in. Or if you're ever in the mood to pamper yourself, we'll hook you up."

"Thank you."

Cooper and I take everything to the front, and he pays for it all. I can't help but take notice of a royal blue lacy number and I promise myself I'll come back later to get it. Surprise Cooper and hopefully knock his socks off.

We leave the store and Cooper puts the purchases in his vehicle before we head back to the shop. He opens the door for me. Beth and Corbin are both with clients, their tattoo guns buzzing away.

I spot a man looking at the tattoo books and I know it's time to get back to reality. Cooper sees him too and kisses my cheek.

"We'll play later," he promises before leaving me to do the job I was hired—kind of—to do.

"Hi, sir," I say. "Welcome to The Ink Spot. Is there something I can help you with?"

When he turns to face me, something nags at my brain. He looks familiar but I can't, for the life of me, place him.

"Nah, I'm just looking." He smiles but it doesn't reach his eyes. He's giving off a creepy vibe and it's only made worse when he looks me up and down and licks his lips. "For now."

22

COOPER

"I'm fine. Really."

I grind my teeth to keep from arguing with her. Lila has given me the same bullshit 'I'm fine' response ever since we returned to the shop. I don't know what happened, but her entire mood shifted, and she won't talk to me. Talk about a double standard. She doesn't want me to shut her out but it's okay if she does it? Fuck that.

"Why won't you talk to me?"

"Because there's nothing to talk about."

Thinking I did something wrong, I try to get answers a different way. "Did I do something at Sandy's that upset you? I'm sorry if I pushed you. That wasn't my intent—"

"You didn't do anything wrong!" she shouts.

"Lila, something is bothering you. Don't tell me it's nothing. Don't tell me you're fine. It's something and you're not."

Lila pushes up off the porch step and starts to pace in the gravel in front of it. She does this for several minutes, huffing and puffing out her frustration, her lips moving as if she's talking to herself.

When she stops, she crosses her arms. "Did you notice that guy that was in the shop when we went back?"

"The one that was looking at the books?" I ask, completely confused and wondering what the hell he has to do with her mood.

"Yeah, him."

I recall the man being there but that's about it. "What about him?"

"Did you see his face?"

I stand up and rest my hands on her shoulders. She's practically vibrating with frustration and that's when I realize that whatever it is that's bothering her isn't something I did. It's something that scared her.

"No, I didn't. Lila, who is he?"

"I don't… I don't know for sure but…" She sighs and drops her chin to stare at the ground.

"Lila?"

"I thought he looked familiar, but I couldn't place him. He creeped me out, kinda looked at me like he was seeing me naked." She shivers. "It was fucking weird. Anyway, he just left, and I thought maybe I imagined it because I really couldn't figure out why I thought I knew him."

"Okay. Did you figure it out?"

"It didn't really hit me until Donovan came to pick up his paycheck."

"Wait. What does Donovan have to do with this?"

"I'm getting to that," she snaps with impatience.

"Would you hurry because I'm confused as hell and all sorts of things are springing to mind?"

"Donovan got his check and left. I remembered that Corbin had asked me to see if Donovan could switch shifts with him one day, so I ran outside because Donovan's car was still in the lot. He didn't see me at first, so I tapped on the window. I leaned in when he rolled it down and he wasn't alone."

"Okay."

"The creepy guy from earlier was in the passenger seat."

"Lila, I need more than that. Donovan can hang out with anyone he wants to. Even creepy customers, although I'll have a talk with him about not bringing him near the shop if he's gonna scare you."

"Coop, when I saw the guy in Donovan's car, it finally clicked. I figured out why he was so familiar. He was there that night, at Drake's."

"Are you saying he—"

"He was one of the guys who beat me."

∽

"Did you really need to call them?"

"Yeah, Lila, I did." The rumble of bikes as everyone arrives is loud and welcoming. We both stand on the porch as they park. "You tell me that one of the guys that beat you was in my shop and you expect me to keep that to myself? Forget the fact that I want to hunt him down and kill him. How about the fact that the BRB would hunt me down and kill *me* if I didn't share this information?"

"You don't want us to kill him, do ya?" Isaiah asks as he walks up the steps.

"No, I guess not."

"Didn't think so."

Isaiah disappears into the cabin and the others follow him. Lila and I are the last to enter, leaving the darkness of the night behind.

"Got any booze in this place?" Noah asks as he helps himself to the bag of chips on the counter.

"Damn, Noah, you've got better manners than that,"

Aiden chastises before he bends and places a kiss on the top of his daughter's head. "Hi, honey."

"Hi, Dad."

"Son, Noah's not wrong. We're gonna need some alcohol for this."

It takes me a minute to move past the term 'son'. I haven't been called that in a very long time and the last time I was, it was by a man I despised. Somehow, hearing it from Aiden feels... right.

"Cooper?"

Lila's hand touches my arm and pulls me from my thoughts.

"They want alcohol."

"Right. Cupboard next to the fridge. I think there's uh, some whiskey and maybe some tequila."

"And you've kept my baby girl away from all of it, right?"

"Yes, sir."

"Shit, son. I'm just giving you a hard time. Lila's old enough to go die for her country so that makes her old enough to have a few drinks every once in a while." Aiden forces a stern look. "Safely, of course."

"Yes, sir."

"Man, you really gotta quit with the 'sir' shit," Isaiah says as he slaps me on the back. "We're all family here. No need for formalities."

Family.

"Told ya." Lila leans into my side and I hold her close. "Acceptance, love, loyalty—"

"And family," I finish for her.

Noah pours shots for everyone and once we all toss them back, Isaiah gets straight down to business.

"So, Lila, tell us what you remember about the guy in the shop."

Lila describes the man with as much detail as she can

remember. She tells them about how she saw Donovan with him and how the guy gave her the creeps.

"If I show you some pictures, would you recognize him?" Liam asks.

"Definitely."

Liam spreads some images out on the table and one jumps out at me.

"Wait a second." I lift up one of the photos and flip it around for everyone to see. "I know this guy."

"That's him," Lila announces at almost the same time. Her face drains of color. "He was in the shop before?"

"Yeah. Came in and said he was referred by a friend. He told me his name was Shawn." I crumple the picture in my fist. "And now I know his *friend*," I use air quotes. "Is Donovan."

"I don't understand," Lila says. "Coop, you hired Donovan when you opened The Ink Spot, right?"

"Yeah, so?"

"So, Donovan has had every opportunity to get to you, to Cammi and Carmen. Hell, he's been alone with both of them."

"Lila, what's your point?" Isaiah asks with fraying patience.

"Hear me out." She starts to pace as she talks her way through her thoughts, trying to make us all understand. "If Donovan is connected to the Knights of Wrath, why wait this long to do something? With as much as they hate Cooper, it doesn't add up. And, if they had such easy access, why even bother with me? No. It just…" She rubs her temples. "It just doesn't make sense. None of it makes any fucking sense."

"Or maybe they just wanna fuck with me and this is the most creative they can get," I snarl.

"No, Lila's right." Aiden's words pull my attention. "Think about it. With Drake, there was a reason behind all of his actions. I'm not saying he was right and I'm not saying I wouldn't kill him with my bare hands if we crossed paths. But to him, he did what he did for a reason. With Donovan, it just doesn't compute." Aiden shifts his attention to Liam. "Tell us what you know about this other mystery guy, VP. Maybe that'll make some of the pieces fit."

"Well, Cooper, he gave you his real name, which was stupid, but whatever." Liam skims through some papers until he finds what he's looking for. He reads the information to everyone. "Shawn Cutter, twenty-nine, New Jersey driver's license, weapon's charge from four years ago, numerous intent to sell charges… that's about it."

"Where in New Jersey?" Pieces are falling into place, but I need to be sure.

"Uh, license says Atlantic City."

"Fuck!"

"What?" Isaiah narrows his eyes in concern.

"Liam, did you dig up any mugshots?"

"I glanced at them, but nothing jumped out at me, so I didn't print them off."

I tip my head to indicate the laptop he brought with him. "Can you hack into police databases with that thing?"

"Does a bear shit in the woods?"

"What?"

"Yes, Cooper, I can hack almost any database with this 'thing.'"

"Great. Pull up his file from the Department of Corrections in Atlantic County. And not the shit that's already public record."

"Kinda figured when you asked if I could hack it," Liam teases.

His fingers fly over the keyboard as he works his magic. My pulse races as I wait for him to get to what I need.

"What specifically are you hoping to find?" Isaiah asks.

I rub my upper arm and grit my teeth. They all know my past, who I am, so why is this so hard?

"Cooper?" Lila prompts.

I lift the sleeve of my shirt to expose my tattoo.

"This."

23

LILA

"I told you not to come in today."

Cooper is pacing the length of the shop and makes no effort to even look at me. I would normally argue with him about how I'm an adult and don't take orders from him but not today. Today is too important.

"You did. I didn't listen."

"I don't want you here for this," he insists.

"I know but I'm here. Besides, we both know how this is gonna play out. Donovan doesn't—"

"Donovan doesn't what?"

Cooper and I both whirl toward the front door. Donovan is standing there with a stupid grin on his face, the same one that always seems to be there. Criminal mastermind, my ass.

"The alarm didn't beep when the door opened," Cooper observes and glares at Donovan. "Why is that?"

"Dude, how am I supposed to know." He walks around the counter, past both of us, and puts his bag down. He looks from Cooper to me and back again. "What?"

"You know what," Cooper snaps.

"No, Cooper, I don't. What the hell is going on?"

"Shawn Cutter."

"Yeah, what about him?"

I watch Donovan closely and he gives away nothing. Either he's a great actor or I'm right and he really doesn't have a clue who he's friends with.

Unfortunately, Cooper is past the point of paying attention to body language and facial expressions. I have no doubt that if I had listened to him and stayed home today, Donovan would already be sprawled out on the floor and no words would have passed between them.

"You tell me."

"Jesus, Cooper. Quit with the cryptic statements and just spit it out."

"Why was Shawn in your car the other day?"

"Pretty sure who I hang out with outside of work is none of your business."

Well, damn. That's not gonna do him any favors.

"Pretty sure when you're hanging out with a guy who beat the shit out of my girlfriend, it's my fucking business."

Donovan visibly flinches at that revelation. His gaze cuts to me and his forehead wrinkles in confusion.

"What's he talking about?" he asks me.

"Talk to me, not her," Cooper snarls.

"Coop," I plead. "Calm down."

Suddenly, the tightly controlled rage explodes, and Cooper whirls on me.

"Don't tell me to calm down! He's involved in this and he knows it. I'll calm down when he pays for what he's done."

I stand my ground. Cooper isn't mad at me and I know he's just lashing out. He can yell all he wants and I can take it.

Donovan snatches up his bag and steps toward the door. "I'm outta here."

Cooper is on him so fast I'd have missed it if I blinked. He throws Donovan back against the wall and pins him there.

"You're not going anywhere. Start fucking talking."

Donovan struggles against Cooper's hold, but it gets him nowhere. Cooper is easily twice his size and add in the adrenaline pumping through him and Donovan's stuck. I can't see Donovan's face, so I stare at Cooper's back. His muscles bunch and twitch beneath his shirt and if it weren't such a volatile situation, it'd be hot as hell.

"How do you know Shawn Cutter?"

"I get my pot from him," Donovan shouts, giving in. It's not at all what I expected him to say. "He came into the shop one day when I was alone. He caught me smoking a joint and struck up a conversation. That's it."

"You've been getting high on my dime?"

"Only a few times, I swear."

"Do you know anything about Shawn, other than he sells pot?"

"No, not really. It's not like we hang out or anything."

"Funny. He's been in a few times when you weren't here and told me that he was referred to me by a 'friend', that he was looking to get a tattoo."

"I don't know anything about that, Cooper. I didn't even know he was here when I wasn't. Dude is weird but he's got good weed."

The tension in Cooper's shoulders eases and his arms fall to his sides. He tips his head back and I imagine he's trying to reign in his temper. I close the distance between me and them, stopping when I'm at their side.

"He does have a tattoo," I tell Donovan.

"Seriously?"

"Yeah, seriously," Cooper says with a bite to his tone. "Looks almost identical to this." Cooper lifts his sleeve.

Donovan's eyes widen. "Knights of Wrath? You're in a gang?"

Oh shit.

Cooper inhales through his nose, very slowly. "Not a gang. And no, not anymore."

"What does this have to do with Shawn?" Donovan looks at me. "Did he really beat you?"

"Yes, he did. And Shawn is also a member of the Knights of Wrath. But he's based out of New Jersey. He's here because of Cooper."

"I'm so confused."

Cooper just stares at him as if trying to figure out if he can be trusted. I believe what Donovan's saying. His words and actions this morning have been stupid, but real.

"Coop, he doesn't know anything." I rest my hand on his forearm. "You know that. He's guilty of being an idiot and a pothead but not of setting us up."

Cooper lowers his head and stares at my hand. He gives a curt nod and breaks away from my touch to pace the length of the shop.

"Can I get to work now?" Donovan asks.

Cooper's laugh is hollow. "Oh, no, you're fired." He stops pacing and stands a few inches from Donovan. "But you get to live so there's that."

"You're firing me? I didn't do anything wrong!"

"You got high while on the job, dumbass," I say when Cooper just stares at him.

"Get out of my shop."

Donovan returns his stare for a moment before he makes his way to the door.

"And Donovan," Cooper calls. "Get your pot somewhere else. I'm pretty sure your life depends on it."

Donovan flips Cooper off before shoving through the door. We both watch as he peels out of the parking lot and I can't help but think that he has no idea how lucky he just got.

"Idiot," Cooper mutters.

"Pretty much. But I believe him that he didn't know about Shawn."

"Me too. He wouldn't have left otherwise."

"Now what?"

Cooper slings an arm around my shoulders and kisses the top of my head.

"Now, we move to Plan B."

24

COOPER

"I know that's not what you wanted to hear."

My fingers tighten around my cell phone and I clench my jaw. I'd called the prosecutor who was involved in the case against the Knights of Wrath to verify that they were all still rotting behind bars and he'd informed me that three of them were released based on their appeals. How in the hell had I not been notified? It's unacceptable.

"One was killed a week after release in a shooting and another overdosed on heroin within two weeks. That leaves Wayne Stanton, a.k.a Screwball. He's got a parole officer and so far, the reports are good."

That only concerns me more. Screwball's road name fits him well. He's got a screw loose and always has something up his sleeve. If it appears that he's doing all the right things that only means he's got something major cooking.

"Oh, wait. What's this?" The sound of rustling papers comes through the line. "He has put in a request to leave the state next week. Something about a sick family member."

My stomach bottoms out. "I'm gonna go out on a limb and say he wants to go to New Jersey."

"Well, yes. Atlantic City. How did you know?"

"Lucky guess."

"Is there something I should know?" the Prosecutor asks.

I could tell him everything and Screwball would be behind bars by the end of the day. But I know that would only be a temporary fix. He got out once and he'll do it again. No, there is only one way to end this for good. Just like Screwball, I've done it once and I can do it again.

"No, nothing," I lie. "I appreciate your time."

I end the call and immediately make another one.

"Hello?"

"Isaiah, it's Cooper."

"Hey man. Lila told me about Donovan. I gotta say, I'm glad the kid isn't involved. One less scumbag to worry about."

"Yeah, it's great. But that's not why I called."

"What's up, brother?"

There it is again, that family reference. It throws me for a loop every time but in a good way.

"I know I'm not a member and it's not exactly protocol, but I'd like to call church. Can we make that happen?"

"Sure. And in case you haven't noticed, we don't always follow your typical MC protocol. If you say we need to meet, we need to meet. No questions asked."

"Thanks, man."

"Don't sweat it. When does this need to happen?"

"Now."

"You got it. We'll meet you in the library."

Isaiah hangs up before I do and I stare at the screen for a moment wondering if this is real, if the BRB is real. I've seen a lot in my life, done a lot, and not much surprises me. But they do. All the time.

Acceptance.

Loyalty.

Brotherhood.

Family.

I race out of the cabin, grateful that Carmen is in school and Cammi and Lila are registering for their next semester. It'll be easier to plan without them present. Because Plan B flew out the window with one phone call and now, we need to figure out Plan C. And probably D and E, too, if the way things are going is any indication.

When I walk into the library ten minutes later, every seat around the table is full. All eyes turn to me and I glance at Isaiah. He waves me over to stand next to him.

"This is your show, brother."

"I don't…" I shake my head. "You're their president."

"Yeah, he is." Liam stands up. "But we don't always follow—"

"Protocol," I finish for him. "He mentioned something like that."

"Cooper, you called this meeting. I already explained that to everyone before you got here. Fill us in on what's going on and we'll go from there."

"Right. Okay."

I scan the faces around the table, each one intense with concentration. I begin to tell them what we learned about Donovan, as well as the information I obtained from the prosecutor about Screwball. No one interrupts and the longer I talk, the more the air thickens with tension.

"I could have told the prosecutor that Screwball isn't going to New Jersey to see family. Not blood family, at least. Hell, maybe I should have. But we all know that it wouldn't have solved anything. No, I want his trip to be approved. I want him to find his way to Indiana. I want Shawn and Drake and every other fuck involved to face me." I pause and pound my fist on the table. "Face us."

Silence follows my speech and I fear I went too far. But

then they start firing questions at me and I can't keep up. A piercing whistle cuts through the noise and they quiet down again.

"One question at a time," Liam says.

"How about we go around the table and you'll all get a turn?" Isaiah asks and when there are nods all around, he continues. "Good. Tillie, you first."

"Is there anything to indicate that Screwball is actually related to the others or is the only connection the MC?"

"No, there's no relation. Screwball was an only child, and his parents are dead. His connection to Shawn is obviously the club. Screwball has been a member for over thirty years, since he was eighteen. The younger members will do anything he asks."

Tillie follows up with another question. "What's the connection to Drake?"

"I can answer that," Liam responds. "I did a little more digging on Shawn and Drake after Cooper verified Shawn's link to the KWMC. Turns out, they're cousins. I can't find anything to indicate that Drake is a member but I'm gonna guess that he's a prospect."

"Makes sense," I concede. The thought that Drake was prospecting had already crossed my mind and it's nice to know I'm not alone in my thinking, even if we can't confirm it.

"Do we know when Screwball is supposed to be heading to New Jersey? Or even if the request will be approved?"

I shift my focus to Isabelle. I haven't had a chance to really get to know her but what I do know, from previous meetings, is she's got a good head on her shoulders and is smart. She's also diabolical when it comes to planning.

"Next week. Not sure of the exact date. And yeah, I think it'll be approved."

"Good. That's what we want."

"It is. But it doesn't leave much time to prepare."

"You're in a room full of veterans, former Navy Seals," Micah chimes in. "We don't need much time."

"My dad's right," Isaiah says. "We'll have everything worked out today, along with several contingencies."

"Okay. Good. Now," I pause and take a deep breath. "Who's going to tell Lila all of this?"

Laughter breaks out and Aiden rises from his seat and comes to slap me on the back.

"Son, that's your problem now."

I certainly don't see Lila as a problem, but her presence could be. I know what I have to do and it's going to be the hardest thing I've ever done. And just like that, with the break of a few promises, all of the happiness I let myself feel will vanish in a cloud of smoke.

Poof.

25

LILA

"What's going on?"

Cooper and Cammi look up from the boxes they're packing, and I can tell Cammi's been crying. Her eyes are red and puffy, and she refuses to meet my gaze. I rush and drop to my knees next to her to wrap her up in a hug. She hangs on to me like her life depends on it.

"Cam, can you give us a minute?"

Cammi pulls away from me and nods at her brother before scrambling to her feet and retreating to the bedroom she uses at the cabin.

"Cooper, what happened?"

He doesn't respond. Instead, he stares at me with eyes that I can only describe as cold and unfeeling. I reach out to touch his arm and he steps back, away from me. Confusion clouds my brain, and a heavy feeling settles in my gut.

"Coo—"

"We're leaving, Lila."

"What?"

"We're going back to our house."

"That's great, Cooper," I exclaim, somehow managing to

have convinced myself that I read the room wrong when I arrived, and this is a good thing.

"Yeah, um, it'll be nice to get home."

Cooper turns away from me and walks to the counter. He leans on his outstretched arms and hangs his head.

"I can go back to my parents and pack my stuff and meet you all there. Maybe grab a pizza on the way."

I'm clinging to an imaginary thread of hope. I know that. The thread doesn't exist. If I'm honest with myself, I knew that the second he opened his mouth, but I want to be wrong. I want that more than I want my next breath.

"You're not going."

"Yes, I am"

Cooper shoves off of the counter and stalks back toward me, looking very much like a predator about to devour its prey. I back up a step, but he grabs me by the arms and gives me a shake.

"Listen to me," he snarls. "You're not going. I don't want you there. Don't push it Lila because I promise you, you won't like what comes out of my mouth if you do."

"Cooper, you're scaring me."

I try to yank free, but he holds me tight. Tears burn at the back of my eyes and I'm powerless to stop them. When one slides down my cheek, Cooper's jaw ticks and his grip tightens.

"You should be scared. I'm a murderer, remember," he sneers.

I shake my head violently, not understanding where this is coming from. The tears fall, unchecked, and my stomach threatens to empty itself of the dinner I ate with my parents not an hour ago.

"You were a convenient distraction." He pushes me away from him and thrusts his hands through his hair. "That's it,

Lila. Do you hear me? A distraction. One that I don't need anymore."

My knees threaten to buckle, and I can't breathe. This can't be happening. What did I do wrong? Everything was fine when I talked to him this morning. I don't understand.

My pain turns to rage, and I force air into my lungs. How dare he do this? I deserve better. So much better. I wipe away the wetness on my cheeks and square my shoulders. I shove everything but the fury out of my mind and advance on him.

"Fuck you, Cooper Long!" I shout. "Fuck you and your issues." His eyes widen for a split second before he narrows them at me. "Fuck. You!"

I turn on my heel and stomp to the door and throw it open. I glance over my shoulder and see him walking toward me. Before he reaches me, I yell one last thing that will hurt him as much as he's hurt me.

"Burn in Hell, Cooper."

I slam the door closed and stand there, chest heaving, anger riding me hard. I lean back against the door and it rattles with what I assume is his fist connecting with the solid wood. I tip my head back and squeeze my eyes shut.

For a second, I wish he'd open the door, tell me this is all a big mistake, but it doesn't happen. The only thing I hear on the other side of the barrier is something sliding against it and a thump when it hits the floor. Cooper, I assume. And then something else catches my ear.

I put my head to the wood and listen hard. He's crying, talking to himself. I strain to hear what he's saying, wishing it didn't matter and pissed because it does.

"Already burning, Sprite. Already burning."

I run. Fast, hard, pushing myself as much as humanly possible to get as far away from the cabin as I can. It's dark out and it isn't long before my lungs are burning from exertion.

I force my legs to slow down and eventually stop to catch my breath. I take in my surroundings and realize that I've run the entire perimeter of the property. Several miles and still, it doesn't feel like it's far enough.

With a glance at my phone, I see that it's getting late and all I want to do is crawl into a bed, any bed, and hide away for days. I take off toward my parents' place to do just that.

As I walk, I think. I analyze. I worry, wish, cry, yell into the wind. How could I be so stupid? Cooper played me like a fiddle. A convenient distraction? Fuck him.

By the time I step onto their porch, I'm angrier than when I left the cabin. I'm so infuriated that I can't even stop myself from slamming the door and when I do, glass shatters on the floor. I glance to my left to see what fell and when my eyes land on the broken picture frame and the photo of my mom at the kitchen sink, I lose it.

I fall to my knees and scramble to pick up the pieces, oblivious to the glass slicing into my palms and the blood dripping onto the floor. Cooper already destroyed me. What's a little more pain?

~

Cooper

"Are you okay?"

I lift my head and look at Cammi. I haven't moved from my spot against the door since Lila stormed out of here. I have no idea how long ago that was, but it might as well have been a lifetime ago.

"No." I shake my head. "Not really."

Cammi sits and leans against the wall next to me, pulling her knees up to her chest. Neither of us speaks for several moments but I know it won't last. It can't last. Even if we don't acknowledge what just happened, life moves on.

"Was that really the only way, Coop? Promise me that was the only way because otherwise, I don't think I can do this."

I put my arm around her shoulders and tuck her into my side. "It's the only way."

"Do I have to like it?"

Her questions break me more than the fight with Lila because they're so reminiscent of the way she sought out my assurance when she was a kid. I hate that she's uncertain. I hate that she's in pain and I'm the cause.

"No, you don't have to like it. I fucking hate it." I rub her arm. "But, kiddo, we need to finish packing. I'd like to head back first thing in the morning. I can't be here any longer than that."

Cammi leans in and kisses my cheek before she stands and goes to her bedroom, leaving me alone with my thoughts. I sit there for a moment longer and then force myself to do what needs to be done. I can't control anything with Lila right now, but I can control the packing.

When I'm almost done, I grab a beer from the fridge, and just as I pop the top, there's a knock on the front door. I stride through the small space to open it, inexplicably hopeful that Lila came back.

"When I said telling Lila was your problem, I didn't mean like this," Aiden barks.

"You know as well as I do that if she stays with me, she's in danger. I did what I had to do to keep her safe."

Aiden's shoulders sag and his face falls. "No, son, you didn't. You just destroyed her quicker than the Knights of Wrath ever could." He pushes past me and goes into the kitchen. "I need a fucking drink."

He lifts the tequila bottle and two shot glasses from the cabinet and pours. He hands one to me and then salutes before he downs it and slams the glass back on the counter. We stare each other down, each waiting for the other to break the silence. I'm the first one to crack.

"How is she?"

I don't have a right to ask but I need to know.

"She's lucky we have Doc, that's how she is."

"What?"

"She came home and when she slammed the door—my baby girl is stronger than she realizes—a picture frame fell and there was broken glass everywhere." He shakes his head. "She didn't even realize she was cutting herself when she was scrambling to pick it up."

"Jesus."

"Anyway, she was so out of it, bleeding and crying, that I had to pick her up and carry her to her room and Scarlett called Doc. He was able to stitch up the cuts and gave her a sedative to help her relax."

"Aiden, I didn't—"

"Don't." He rests his hand on my shoulder. "I'm not the one you need to explain things to. My daughter is."

I look away and begin to pace. I never meant for any of this to happen. I knew my words would hurt but Lila's strong and I thought she'd yell and cry and move on. I also never meant to fall in love with her but here I am.

So completely in love with the woman I just crushed, and I can't do a damn thing about it. Not yet.

"There's nothing I can say to change your mind, is there? You're determined to see this thing through and leave her in the dark?"

"Yes, I'm going to see this through first. But I promise you, I will make it right."

"And what am I supposed to do, huh? I have to admit, I'm torn, Cooper. As a father and as a man, a brother."

"Can I ask you something?"

"Of course."

"If this were Scarlett, what would you do differently than me?"

Aiden heaves a sigh and shakes his head. "Son, if this were Scarlett, not a damn thing."

"Exactly. You were at the same meeting as I was. We have a solid plan, and it will work. But Lila can't be a part of it. I won't risk her for anything. I'd rather she hates me for a week and be alive. Hell, I'd rather she hates me forever and still be breathing."

"I hope for her sake, and yours, that a week is all it takes."

"It will be. You'll see. I know Screwball and he's not going to drag this out. He can't. In his mind, his reputation with the club depends on it."

26

LILA

One month later...

"That's the last of it."

I wipe the sweat off my forehead and then prop my hands on my hips to survey the mess that is my new home. Boxes are scattered through the small living room and I know that I have a long few days ahead of me getting everything unpacked and put away. Not to mention the IKEA furniture that needs put together.

"Thanks, mom. I really appreciate all your help." I give her a hug and then turn to my sister. "You too, Tillie."

"Anytime. And your dad, Micah, and Isaiah will be here tomorrow to help with the furniture."

"And no doubt lectures about how I should have stayed home."

I've been hearing the same thing for the last two weeks, ever since I announced that I found an apartment near campus and was moving out. No matter how many times I tried to explain that I couldn't stay at my parent's house anymore, it didn't matter. Living under their roof, being on that property, driving past the main house and seeing Cooper's Harley parked there gutted me. It was torture and I had to end it.

Tillie and my mom exchange a look, but I ignore it. I've seen it happen too many times in the last month to give a shit anymore what it's about. In fact, it's not just them. It's everyone. Like they all know something that I don't. Hell, maybe they do, but it doesn't matter. I'm free and can finally move on and put Cooper firmly where he belongs: in the rearview mirror of life.

"Still haven't heard from Cammi?" Tillie asks.

I snort. "Nope. I quit trying to call her. She never answers anyway. And she hasn't been in class at all." I force a smile. "Good riddance."

"You don't mean that, honey."

"Yeah, mom, I do. She was supposed to be my best friend. I get that Cooper's her brother, but I never thought she'd ghost me if things didn't work out."

"Maybe she just doesn't know what to say," Tillie suggests.

"Maybe," I concede. "Anyway, it's fine." And because I'm a glutton for punishment, I ask the one question that's always on my mind no matter how hard I try to pretend otherwise. "How's Coop doing?"

"As a prospect or in general?"

"As a prospect," I clarify because I definitely don't care how he is in general.

Bullshit Lila Rose. You care. A lot.

"Really good." Tillie smiles. "He fits in great, although Dad gives him the evil eye every chance he gets. They're still trying to sort out some things on a case that popped up after he left the cabin. I won't bore you with the details."

I roll my eyes at her. She says that every time the club is brought up or a case is mentioned. I know I told them all that I needed some space and that I wanted to figure out who I am without the club, but I didn't mean that I never wanted to know anything.

Mom glances at her phone and then sighs. "Honey, I'm sorry, but we have to get back."

"I know." I hug them both again. "Go. I'll be fine. I'm gonna unpack a few boxes, get my TV set up and then kick back for the night. The rest of it can wait until tomorrow."

"You're sure you have enough food and everything?"

"I'm fine, mom. I promise."

She reaches into her purse, pulls out a twenty and hands it to me. "Order yourself a pizza or something."

"You better take it," Tillie teases. "Or we're gonna be here all night and you don't want that."

"Fine." I snatch the bill. "Thanks. Love you guys."

"Love you too."

I lock the door behind them and lean against it to once again survey my apartment. So much to do and no energy to do any of it. Tears well in my eyes but I refuse to let them fall. This is what I wanted. Space. Independence. A life outside of the club.

But you never wanted to be alone.

I force away my wayward thoughts and push up my sleeves. I may not have any energy, but hard work is exactly what I need to take my mind off of things. I grab the box cutter from the toolbox on the floor and start opening boxes.

Six hours and an extra cheese pizza later, my living room resembles an actual living room. I flop down on the new couch and turn on the TV. Netflix is calling my name. I get all of my account details entered and wait for them to be verified. Once they are, I click on the first action movie that pops up and hit 'play'.

Exhaustion sets in and I struggle to keep my eyes open. Before I can fall asleep, I get up and double-check all the locks to assure myself that I'm safe and secure. Just as I lay back down on the couch, my cell phone buzzes with a notification. I ignore it.

When it buzzes again, and then again, I snag it off the coffee table and look at the screen. The notifications are for news alerts that I set up on Facebook. I click on them and read the first headline that pops up.

College Junior with Suspected Gang Ties Found Dead in Alley

The other headlines are similar. I open one of the news articles and a picture of Drake stares back at me from the screen. They managed to find a decent picture of him, and he doesn't look like the evil son of a bitch I came to know. Although, I've learned the hard way that good looks do not equal a good person.

I skim the article but don't learn much. What I do know is this: Drake's body was found in an alley, in downtown Indianapolis, with several gunshot wounds and an unidentified object jammed down his throat.

I swipe away from that article to look at the others. The only other detail that they provide me with is that the coroner can't work out an official time of death other than to say that Drake had been dead 'a while' before his body was discovered.

Bile climbs up the back of my throat. I rush to the bathroom and make it to the toilet in time to lose my dinner. When the heaving stops, I blindly reach for a towel and then remember that they're still packed. I pull my t-shirt over my head and wipe my mouth clean on that before digging through boxes to find what I need.

It takes a half-hour, but I finally find the towels, toothbrush and toothpaste, and everything I need to get a shower. I spend another half hour scrubbing myself clean. I stumble around the apartment in my towel to find clothes and end up settling on a pair of panties and a clean t-shirt.

Back on the couch, I wrap myself up in my blanket and reach for my cell. I pull up my text messages and my thumb hovers over Cooper's name. The last message from him is partially visible and tears sprint to my eyes as I read it.

> **Can't wait to see you tonight. Bring the stuff from…**

The rest of the text is hidden in the preview. It doesn't matter. I know what it says. What was supposed to be a fun night of exploring our purchases from Sandy's Lingerie turned into one of the worst nights of my life.

He deserves to know about Drake.

He may deserve to know but do I have to be the one to tell him? I know the answer: no. But it doesn't seem to matter. I open the full text screen and type a few words.

> **Drake is dead**

I hit send before I can talk myself out of it. There. It's done. He knows. *Now* I can really put him in that rearview mirror.

27

COOPER

"It had to be Screwball."

I skim through the autopsy report that Liam managed to get and immediately see why Screwball is the first person to come to mind. After I got the text from Lila, and after I sobered up enough to read, I pulled up everything I could find online about Drake's death. At the time, what stood out to me was that an object was jammed in his throat but none of the reports said what it was. The autopsy does.

"Yeah, it's him." I slam the document down on the table, rattling the coffee mugs of the other brothers. "He's the only one I know who shoves screwdrivers down the throats of his victims… before he kills them."

"Damn, Coop," Liam whistles. "How did you turn out so normal after growing up around these fucks?"

"I'm feeling anything but normal."

"This is good though," Aiden chimes in. "One bad guy down and we didn't have to lift a finger."

"True enough," Isaiah agrees. "But I don't like it. It's been one thing after another for the last month and none of it is stuff we could have predicted. I certainly never thought we'd still be here, a month later, trying to figure this out. We're on what? Plan Y by now?"

"Look, guys, I'm sorry about all of this," I say with sincerity. "This is not what you signed up for. Fuck, it's not at all what I was expecting when I made Lila hate me. One week. That's what I thought." I look at Aiden. "That's what I told you and now look at where we're at. She still hates me and she's living on her own, Drake is dead, Screwball is in jail for a parole violation but still pulling strings on the outside, and we can't find Shawn Cutter to save our lives."

"Son, save it," Aiden snaps. "None of us blame you and we see this through till the end. When we agreed to help and then when you started prospecting, we all knew the risks. There's not a man, or woman, at this table that doesn't understand that shit can go sideways real quick. Stop beating yourself up about it." He grins. "As for Lila, she's covered. Do you really think I was gonna let my baby girl go off on her own without making sure she was protected?" He laughs. "We've got someone on her at all times. Trust me, she'll never know they're there."

"She's gonna hate you when she finds out," I point out to him.

He shrugs. "I'm taking a page out of your book. Do what needs doing to keep her safe."

"Touché, old man," I chuckle.

"Anyway," Aiden continues. "We've got a schedule already in place as far as Lila's protection detail goes. What we really need to do is find Shawn Cutter. Screwball may be responsible for Drake's death, but he didn't get his hands dirty doing it. Not from a cell."

"I may have an idea about that," Liam says, and all eyes turn to him. "Let's use Donovan to lure him out."

"I don't think he's gonna be in a cooperating mood, especially if it means doing something for me. I fired him, remember?"

"We don't have to give him a choice in the matter," Isaiah counters, and when the others begin to protest, he holds a hand up to silence them. "This isn't exactly our normal type of case so I don't think we can play it normal."

"If we cross this line then where do we draw the new one?" Micah asks his son. "I'm not saying this isn't the right move, but I want to make sure we aren't going down a road we can't return from."

"I hear ya, Pops," Isaiah assures him. "And if I thought we were going to be doing something that would jeopardize the club, I wouldn't suggest it, let alone follow through. I think, in this particular case, we need to stop thinking like the Broken Rebel Brotherhood and really treat it like a mission, like a military operation."

Micah nods, as do the others, silently agreeing with our President.

"If we can get Donovan to help, what exactly would he be doing?" I ask, knowing this is one of the only options left but still having no real clue as to how it would work.

"Donovan told you that he was getting his pot from Shawn, so we use that," Liam explains. "I think we can all agree that it was Shawn that killed Drake for Screwball. They may have been cousins but from what we know about the Knights of Wrath, blood family doesn't mean shit. I think we can also all agree that a sale of a little bit of pot isn't gonna interest Shawn. He was selling it to Donovan before because that was his way of getting close to you, Cooper."

"I'm with you so far."

"What if Donovan 'brokers' a deal between Shawn and a buyer for large quantities of heroin? You said that the Knights of Wrath run drugs so something like that would interest them. It would also bring Shawn in close proximity with Donovan which means, in his mind, he's wide open to eliminate that loose end."

"That all sounds great, as far as bringing Shawn out into the open, but how does it solve our Screwball issue? How does it end this so that I'm safe, my sisters are safe?"

"That's where things get a little tricky," Liam says.

He spends the next hour laying out his idea, only stopping when someone asks a question. By the time yet another plan is formed, I'm still not convinced it'll work. But I'm willing to try anything.

"We need a few days to get things set up and to get Donovan on board," Isaiah remarks before ending the meeting. "You all know what you need to do. Once we have Donovan's cooperation, we'll meet again to finalize everything. For now, get to work."

Members file out of the library while Isaiah and Liam remain at the table, talking quietly. I debate on sticking around but decide against it. All I want to do is go home and forget, even if only for a little while.

I make my way out to my Harley and fire it up but before I can take off, Isaiah steps out onto the porch and calls me back in. I heave a sigh, frustrated at not being able to refuse. As a prospect, if he wants me to do something, I do it.

"What's up?" I ask when I'm at his side.

"Liam and I want to talk to you."

A knot forms in my gut. Did I do something wrong? What if they tell me they've changed their minds and they aren't gonna see this through? What if they say that there was a vote and I'm out?

I follow Isaiah back into the library, my thoughts churning and every fear and insecurity rearing its ugly head. Liam is leaning against the table, arms crossed over his chest, but he relaxes his stance and a shit-eating grin spreads when he sees me.

"Dude, when was the last time you got out? And not for work or club business? Just for fun."

I shrug. I'm not about to admit that the last time was with Lila. They aren't stupid men. They know.

"We're taking you to Dusty's. I'm tired of watching you mope around." Isaiah claps me on the back. "The girls are already here so you can't use them as an excuse. You need to relax. We've got a lot of work ahead of us but for tonight, you're gonna put it out of your mind and have a few beers with friends."

"I'm not really in the mood to be social," I argue, although I know it does me no good. It's written all over their faces that they aren't going to back down.

"And we don't really care," Liam states. "C'mon. Give us two hours. If you still want to go home and punish yourself about Lila and all the rest of it in two hours, I'll drive you there myself and set you up with as much booze as you can want to shut the world out."

Two hours. I can do that. I don't want to, but I can.

"Fine. But be prepared to be buying a lot of alcohol on the way home."

They both laugh at me and I realize that this is something else I've missed out on. Friends that give a shit about me and not just because of what I can do for them or a club. It's nice. Annoying as hell right now, but nice.

When we arrive at Dusty's, it isn't busy at all. There are a few customers sitting at the bar, nursing beers, and only two tables are taken by others who are eating. I've been here when the place is packed so it surprises me that it's this dead, but I'm grateful for it. Fewer people to piss me off.

"Hey guys," Ruby, the bartender, calls out. "What brings you in tonight?"

"Trying to get this fool to forget about Lila for a while,"

Liam answers as he slides onto a stool. "Three beers and three shots of Jack, please."

"You got it." Ruby makes quick work of getting the drinks ready and when she hands one to me, she smiles. "Cooper, why don't you just call her? Lila's good people. If you explain why you did what you did, she'll understand."

I down the shot in front of me, briefly wondering how she knows what I did to Lila. I certainly didn't tell her. And then, out of the corner of my eye, I see Liam give a slight shake of his head at her. Huh. So, Liam told her. I don't care that he did, but I find it interesting that they're close enough that he shares that kind of information with her. I glance at Isaiah and he seems to be oblivious to the exchange. Instead, he's focusing on his cell, no doubt texting Tillie, just to check in.

"Is there something going on between the two of you?" I ask, hoping to steer the conversation in any other direction other than Lila.

"What?" Liam balks. "No."

Ruby makes a mock gagging sound. "No, definitely not."

Their words match but neither of them is telling the truth. At the very least, they're fucking.

"Whatever you say." I push my empty shot glass forward. "Can I get another?

Ruby pours and I drink. This keeps up for the entire two hours. Pour, drink, pour, drink. Isaiah and Liam talked me into several games of pool, but I had to quit because not only was I getting my ass handed to me, but I'm also not very steady on my feet. I'm numb though and that's something.

"Two hours are up," Liam announces. "Are we taking you home or staying?"

"One more drink and then home," I say, slurring my words. "But not my home. Lila's home. I want to see Lila."

"Brother, I don't think that's a good idea," Isaiah says. "You're drunk and nothing good can come of that."

"It's a great idea," I argue. "One of my best."

"Hardly," Isaiah snorts. "If we take you, then what? Do you really think she's gonna let you in?"

No.

"Yes."

"Okay, for the sake of argument, let's say she does let you in," Liam states philosophically. "What are you gonna do? You're not exactly firing on all cylinders so I'm pretty sure any meaningful conversation is out of the question. What? You just want to pass out on her couch and piss her off?"

They're right, of course, but I don't care. "She can slam the door in my face and it wouldn't matter. I'll take it if it means I can get even a split-second glimpse of her."

"You are so far gone it's not even funny," Isaiah observes. "Look, I'm open to this insane idea. I think you were an idiot for sending her away in the first place. But I have one condition."

"Are you nuts?" Liam asks him, eyes wide. "This isn't going to end well, and Tillie will kill you if she finds out you were involved."

"Nah," Isaiah assures him. "I'll just tell her that I did it for love. Tillie's a shark when she has to be but when it comes to matters of the heart, she's a softy. She'll understand."

"Who said anything about love?" I demand, focusing on that one word.

"Brother, you love Lila, and you know it. The sooner you accept that, the sooner you tell her that, at least some of your life can go back to normal."

"What was your condition?" I ask, trying to steer the conversation away from my feelings.

"It's simple. If, by some miracle, she doesn't send you packing, you don't push her away again. Don't shut her out."

I open my mouth to protest but he just keeps talking. "I get why you did it. I really do. But it hasn't done either of you any favors and nothing has worked out the way we wanted. This was never supposed to go on this long. And now Lila's distancing herself from her family, her home, all because she's hurt. I don't like it." He takes a deep breath. "Cooper, you need to be all in. No more calling the shots with her because you think it's what's best for her. No more pushing her away and shutting her out. All in or nothing. No more in between."

I give myself a few minutes to consider what he's saying. I stand by what I did with Lila, even if it's turned my life upside down. I did the right thing, but it was only the right thing at the time, when a week was all it was supposed to be.

Is it still the right thing? Will it be the right thing in another month, a year, a decade?

The answer is simple: no. Being without Lila isn't right. Doing the wrong thing for the right reasons isn't any way to live. Hell, I'm not even really living, not without her.

I look at Isaiah with certainty, more certainty than I've ever felt.

"I'm all in."

28

LILA

I bolt upright and reach for the light beside my bed. I was having a really good dream but a noise that didn't belong pulled me from my deep sleep. I glance around my room but see nothing that could be responsible. I listen for a moment and hear nothing.

I scoot up the mattress and lean against the headboard. I'm losing my mind. Ever since learning of Drake's murder yesterday, I've been jumpy. Seeing shadows when there are none. Hearing things when—

Thwack... thwack... thwack.

I throw the covers from my body and jump out of bed. I knew I heard something. I peak around my door frame, searching for the source. Other than boxes, there's nothing.

"Lila, open up!"

What the hell?

I rush to the door and stand on my tiptoes to look through the peephole. My breath hitches and I step back as if hit with a taser. You've got to be kidding me.

"I'm not going anywhere so you might as well open up."

Anger rushes to the surface and I unlock the door and yank it open.

"What the hell do you want, Cooper?"

He's bracing his arms on either side of the door, leaning forward like he hasn't a care in the world. His grin causes his dimples to wink at me, almost making me forget that I'm supposed to hate him.

"This."

I cross my arms over my chest and glare at him. "What? To scare the shit out of me in the middle of the night and wake my neighbors?"

"Nope." His grin slips but only for a second. "I wanted to see you." His gaze travels the length of my body from my face to my toes and back up again. "Fuck, you're pretty."

"Are you drunk?"

He nods slowly. "Little bit."

I lean to the side to look past him into the night. Isaiah and Liam are standing next to Liam's Jeep in the complex parking lot and when they see me, they both wave.

"I'll kill 'em," I mumble.

"Don't kill 'em. I made 'em bring me."

"Fine. Then make them take you away."

I try to slam the door in his face, but he flattens his palm against it to stop me.

"C'mon, Sprite, let me in."

"Why the hell should I? You wanted nothing to do with me, remember?"

Cooper's drunken playfulness disappears, and he hangs his head. I ignore the voice in my head, the one screaming at me that this is what I wanted. For him to come to me, for him to want me. I ignore the pang in my chest at the defeated set of shoulders.

He lifts his head and locks eyes with me and the pain I see reflected in them, I find impossible to ignore. "I didn't mean a word of it, Lila. Please, give me a few minutes to explain. If you still want me to leave after that I will. And you'll never have to see me again."

I start to waver but refuse to give in so easily. No, he needs to squirm just a little bit. "You say you didn't mean it but how am I supposed to believe you? You've lied to me. I just don't know if it was then or if it's right now."

"I'm not lying. Not now."

"I repeat, why should I believe you?"

"Because, Sprite, I love you."

The words might as well be a physical blow because I stumble back a few steps. Seriously? This is how he wants to play this? Mess with my emotions, toy with my heart just a little bit longer? Use me as a distraction for whatever the hell caused him to seek out oblivion at the bottom of a bottle?

And if he is telling the truth and he loves you? Then what, Lila Rose?

I know I should make him leave, tell the guys to get him the hell outta here. I know I shouldn't open myself up again and risk my heart. I *know* these things and still, find myself stepping to the side and inviting him in, almost as if I have no control over my body.

He stares for a moment before recognizing the chance I'm giving him and stepping inside. I close the door behind him and flip the lock. Cooper looks around the room and the more boxes his eyes land on, the stormier his expression gets.

"Why did you move?"

The question startles me but only because the answer is one I still haven't fully accepted.

"To be closer to campus," I lie.

"Bullshit." He sees right through me and it's unsettling. "Honesty goes both ways, Lila."

I snap. "You don't get to do that, Coop. You don't get to worm your way into my apartment in the middle of the night based on a lie and then get all sanctimonious because you think I'm lying."

"But you *are* lying, aren't you?"

"You said you wanted to explain why you pushed me away," I remind him. "Explain or leave. Those are your options."

Cooper moves to the couch and sits down. I vibrate with frustration but keep it in check. The less I argue with him, the quicker we can get through this and he can leave.

Is that what you want? For him to leave? He said he loves you.

Those questions and more ping pong around in my skull. In an effort to give myself a chance to calm down, I go to the kitchen and get a couple bottles of water out of the refrigerator. I return to the living room and stop dead in my tracks.

Cooper's head has flopped onto the back of the couch and he's passed the fuck out. So much for getting through this and him leaving. I could wake him and make him go but there's something about the vulnerability of it all that keeps me from doing that.

The last month has been a waking nightmare. It's been torture of the worst kind and I'm tired of it. I want answers. I want to know why he did what he did. I want to know if he meant it when he said he loves me. I want *him*.

Mind made up, I set the bottle of water on the coffee table and pull the blanket off the back of the couch to cover him. He shifts slightly but doesn't wake. I watch him for a few more minutes, mind swirling with emotion, and then go to my room and close the door.

Morning. I'll get my answers first thing in the morning.

∽

I'm gonna strangle his stupid, hungover ass.

I roll over in bed and pull the covers over my head. Just

because he's awake, and hopefully with a miserable headache, doesn't mean he's gotta be loud as hell and drag me down with him.

The banging that woke me up doesn't stop so I climb out of bed and storm out into the living room, determined to give him a piece of my mind. Cooper is still passed out on the couch and the banging continues. I realize it's someone knocking and my anger skyrockets.

I'm tired and pissed off so I yank the door open while demanding, "What the hell do you—"

Two police officers are standing on the other side and my stomach drops.

"Ma'am, I'm Officer Kinney and this is my partner, Officer Banton."

Both men force polite smiles, and it grates on my nerves. "What can I help you with, officers?"

"We're conducting a murder investigation and…"

Officer Kinney's words fade away. Murder investigation? This has to be about Drake. But why are they here, wanting to talk to me? I may have wanted him dead but I sure as hell didn't kill him. They can't possibly think that.

"Ma'am?"

I shake my head and refocus on the offers. "Sorry, what did you say?"

"Is he here?"

"Who?" I really should have paid attention to what they were saying.

"Mr. Long… Cooper Long. Is he here?"

"I'm Cooper Long."

I whirl around and see Cooper standing next to the couch. His lips are set in a thin line and his body is taut with tension.

Before I know what's happening, Officer Banton brushes past me and pulls a pair of handcuffs from his duty belt.

"Cooper Long, you're under arrest for the murder of Drake Stine." Officer Kinney begins as Banton yanks Cooper's hands behind his back and slaps the cuffs on.

"You can't be serious?" I shout. "Cooper didn't murder anyone. You've got this all wrong."

"Lila, calm down," Cooper instructs.

"Calm down!" I shriek. "You're being arrested for murder, Coop. That's not something to be calm about."

"Ma'am, I need you to step aside and let us do our job." Officer Kinney's tone is firm but kind.

"You're doing your job wrong!"

"Lila," Cooper snaps to get my attention. "It's fine. I'll be fine. Call Isaiah and tell him what's happening. He'll know what to do."

Tears stream down my cheeks, which feel like they're on fire with outrage. I can only nod at him.

As Cooper is led from my apartment, he calls over his shoulder. "Remember what I told you last night, Sprite? Don't ever forget that."

Officer Banton walks Cooper to the patrol car as Officer Kinney reads him his rights. I stand there, equal parts horrified and furious. I watch as they drive away, the back of Cooper's head visible through the rear window.

"I love you too, Coop," I whisper when the vehicle is out of sight.

29

COOPER

"You're not doing yourself any favors, Mr. Long."

I stare at the officers across the table from me. I tried to answer their questions but after four hours of talking, I'm done. They have their minds made up. Of course, it doesn't help that my fingerprints were found on the screwdriver in Drake's throat. At least, according to them. I have no idea how they would have gotten there.

"I don't know how to convince you that I was framed."

"Do you know how many times we hear that?" Officer Kinney leans back in his chair. "Too many to count."

"Just tell us what happened, and we'll tell the prosecutor you cooperated. I'm sure he'd be willing to strike a deal."

"I don't want a deal." I flatten my cuffed hands on the table. "I'm done talking. I want my attorney."

"Now, you know as well as I do that our hands will be tied once your attorney gets here. That deal we mentioned probably won't happen if we have to—"

The door to the interrogation room swings open and Tillie steps inside. "Gentleman." She closes the door behind her and steps up to the table to set her bag down. "I believe my client asked for his attorney."

Both officers rise to their feet with expressions that remind me of a kid with his hand caught in the cookie jar.

"Miss Winters, this isn't usually your kinda case," Officer Banton observes.

"No, it's not. But it doesn't change the facts. I *am* Mr. Long's attorney and Mr. Long *is* innocent."

"I'm sure you'll feel differently once you see the evidence."

"I assure you, I won't." Tillie opens her bag and pulls out a two-inch binder, one I recognize. "But you might, once you read this." She drops the binder so it thuds against the table to punctuate her claim.

"What's that?" Officer Kinney asks as he reaches for the binder.

Tillie slides it out of his reach and the smile on her face reminds me of a viper messing with its target. "May I have a minute alone with my client?"

Even these two know when they're out of cards to play. "Sure."

When the door closes behind them, Tillie sags against her chair. "God, they're assholes."

"Tell me about it."

She rolls her neck and looks at me. "So, did you work things out with my sister?"

"That's your first question to me?" I ask incredulously.

"Of course it is. Family comes first."

"Right." I shake my head. "No, we didn't work things out. In case you missed the memo, I was arrested for murder."

With a flick of the wrist, Tillie dismisses my sarcastic remark. "I didn't miss it. Clearly."

"Why didn't you let them see the binder? It's got everything we have on Screwball, Drake, and Shawn."

"It does but I want to see what they have first."

"And I want to go home."

"I know you do but we have a plan."

"You've gotta be fucking kidding me!" I shout as my fist connects with the table. "How many more plans are we going to cycle through before this is over? Get me outta here and we can still carry out—"

"Is everything okay in here?" Officer Kinney opens the door and asks.

"Everything is fine, Tom," Tillie responds. "Thanks."

When he's gone, I lean close and in a harsh whisper, finish my thought. "We'll carry out the plan with Donovan. But I can't do it from here. Oh, and there's the pesky little detail about me being innocent."

Tillie studies me for a minute and I feel the urge to squirm in my seat under her scrutiny.

"Lila likes this plan."

"That's not fair," I accuse.

Tillie shrugs. "Maybe not but Isaiah told me to remind you that you're all in." She rests a hand atop one of mine. "Cooper, this is it. Just a few more days and it will all be over. You just have to put your trust in us as much as we have in you."

I do trust them. All of them. I wouldn't be prospecting otherwise. But I feel like a puppet where, no matter how hard I try to cut the strings, I can't and everyone else continues to pull them.

"What about Cammi and Carmen? If I'm in here, where will they be?"

"They're still at the main house. They're aware of what's going on. And before you can argue, remember, this involves them too. Cooper, the world is full of bad guys. That's not anything new to your sisters. This way, they get to see the good guys win."

"It's not that simple."

"No, it's not, but I know what it's like to be lied to and kept in the dark. I don't want that for them."

"Fine. It's done now."

"Yeah, it is," Tillie agrees. She straightens in her chair. "So, do you want to hear the plan or not?"

"What choice do I have?"

"There's always a choice, Cooper. If you don't want to hear it and you just want to go home to wait for the next shit pile to hit the fan, that's your call. I'll do that. I'll get you out of here today." She opens the binder and shows me a mugshot of Screwball. "But, if you can see past your fear and anger, even for a few minutes, I'll explain to you exactly what's going to happen and when you do get out of here in a few days, you'll never have to worry about this asshole, ever again. It'll be over. Really over."

I thought it was over when I left Nevada. I thought it was over for seven years. I don't think I can go another day without a light at the end of the tunnel. I need this. My sisters need this. And if it doesn't work, we'll run. Again.

"What's the plan?"

An hour later, Tillie leaves the interrogation room to find the officers. When the three of them return, I know Tillie already started to lay the groundwork. Kinney and Banton are both sporting gloating grins. They think they're about to close the book on a murder case. Little do they know.

Tillie returns to the chair next to me. She grabs the binder off the table and puts it in her bag. Everything that's needed to prove my innocence disappears from view and it's hard to remember that it's a good thing. It's the plan.

Officer Banton places a recorder in the middle of the table and depresses the button. "Mr. Long, your attorney tells us that you're refusing to turn over the information that would exonerate you. Is that true?"

"Yes."

"Care to tell us why?"

"No."

"Do you want to hear my theory?" Officer Kinney asks.

I glance at Tillie and she nods. "Sure." I shrug. "Why not?"

"I think you're full of shit. I think you killed Drake Stine and you, along with your attorney, are stalling. There isn't a lick of evidence pointing to anyone other than you for this murder and they're never will be."

"I think that concludes this interview," Tillie says with authority and stands, slinging her bag over her shoulder as she does.

"We're not done," Officer Banton complains.

"Yes, we are. I have another meeting I need to get to, and my client won't be talking without me present." Tillie turns to me. "Do you need anything, Cooper?"

I need a whole helluva lot.

"No."

"Alright then. I'll be back tomorrow, and we'll discuss your defense."

With that, she leaves, pulling the door closed behind her. Kinney and Banton are speechless and it takes all of my willpower not to laugh at their shocked expressions. It's clear they weren't expecting how this played out and now they have no idea what to do next.

It would seem that Tillie, much like Lila, is a firecracker.

30

LILA

"What if this doesn't work?"

I bump Cammi's shoulder with mine. I missed having her in my life for the last month and I wish like hell we hadn't been thrust together again under these circumstances, but I am happy to have her back. Now we just need to get her brother out of the fucking slammer, and all will be right in the world.

"It will, Cam." What I don't say is it has to work. Because if it doesn't, there's a very real chance that *I'll* be the one sitting in a cell awaiting trial for murder.

"How do you know?"

"Listen to me, okay." She nods. "The Broken Rebel Brotherhood is the best. And I don't just mean this chapter when I say that. We've got chapters all over the country and they've got our back with this. It's been a crazy few days but everything is in place, everyone is where they're supposed to be. It's going to work."

"It's time to go."

I lift my head and see Isaiah standing in the doorway. I give Cammi a hug and kiss her cheek. "See ya later."

I follow Isaiah outside, where Tillie is waiting in the car. I get in the backseat and put on my seatbelt. My heart is racing, my hands are shaking, and no amount of deep breathing is helping.

Tillie spins in the passenger seat so she's facing me. "Do you want to go over everything one last time?"

"No." I shake my head. "I've got it."

"The transport plane landed this morning. Pops spoke with Jackson Stark and confirmed that he and Slade were on board and everything is on track." Isaiah navigates the highway as he reassures me. "Jackson also confirmed that Jett was able to pull some strings with his former DEA contacts. The DEA agreed to let Jett assist. And I talked to the Vegas and Atlantic City chapter presidents and they're all set."

Knowing that we've got the very people that have helped so much in the past eases some of my worry. Not all of it, but enough that I feel like I can breathe again.

"And Shawn?" I ask because he's been the one loose end in all of this.

"Noah, Liam, and Jace are with Donovan handling that."

"Good."

"You remember everything I told you about the arrest process?" Tillie asks, concern etched in the lines of her face. "I can go over it again if you want."

"I'm fine," I snap.

"Okay." Tillie faces forward.

"Til, I'm sorry." I heave a sigh. "I'm nervous but I'm fine. Knowing that everyone else is good to go helps a lot." It hits me that there's one person Isaiah didn't mention. "Hey, what about Cooper? Did you talk with him today?"

"Of course. As his attorney, I met with him briefly."

"And he's good?"

"He knows what he has to do."

"But is he good?"

Tillie glances over her shoulder and smiles. "He's fine. He's anxious to see you. And his sisters."

I smooth my hands over my thighs to wipe the sweat off. "Not too long now."

"Nope." Isaiah exits the highway and turns left, toward the police station. "We'll be there in ten minutes. Any last questions?"

I shake my head vigorously.

We remain silent for the remainder of the drive. When Isaiah pulls into the parking lot, an eerie calm washes over me. I can do this. I've wanted to be treated like an adult for so long and this is the most adult thing I've ever done. I've been handed my wings, mended and stronger than ever, and now it's time to fly.

I enter the building and Tillie is a few steps behind me. Together but separate. I go to one end of the counter and she goes to the other, two-inch binder in hand.

"How can I help you?" the woman behind the desk asks me at the same time another woman asks Tillie the same thing.

"I killed Drake Stine." My voice is strong, confident.

"I'm here to give Officer's Kinney and Banton information regarding the Drake Stine murder," Tillie responds at the same time.

And exactly as expected, we're both led into an interrogation room.

~

Cooper

I glance at the clock on the wall.

What is taking so long?

I should have been out of here by now, not leaning

against a cinderblock wall with all sorts of awful scenarios running through my head.

"Long!"

I push off the wall and walk toward the guard who summoned me.

"Your attorney's here… again."

It's about damn time.

"Okay."

The guard leads me through the halls of the jail and through the underground tunnel that connects it to the police station where I'll meet with Tillie. And Lila if everything is going according to plan.

We stop in front of the same room I met with Tillie in earlier. I can see Lila through the glass panel in the door and she's in deep conversation with Tillie. Turning my head toward the sound of footsteps, I see Officer's Kinney and Banton striding down the hall, both carrying large stacks of documents.

"It's your lucky day, Long." Kinney opens the door and urges me inside before turning to the guard that brought me over from the jail. "You can go back. He won't be returning."

With the guard summarily dismissed, we all crowd around the table, which now has a recorder in the center.

"Miss Winters, we've reviewed the information provided. We also shared it with the prosecutor and all charges against Mr. Long are being dropped."

"That's good news, gentlemen." Tillie flicks a glance toward my hands. "Can we get those damn cuffs off of him then?"

Officer Banton removes the cuffs and immediately steps toward Lila. Lila's eyes grow wide and my heart twists. We all knew this was coming but it doesn't make it any easier.

"Lila Winters, you're under arrest for the murder of—"

"Not so fast," Tillie interrupts. "My client didn't murder anyone."

Kinney and Banton exchange confused looks. "We know, Miss Winters. I believe we just established that," Kinney says.

"I'm sorry, I misspoke." Tillie flashes a million-dollar smile. "*Neither* of my clients have murdered anyone."

"Tillie," Officer Banton huffs out an angry breath. "Lila confessed to killing Mr. Stine."

"That's correct. My client, Lila Winters, did in fact kill Drake Stine."

"Then let me do my job."

"She killed him in self-defense." Tillie pulls another folder out of the bag at her feet. "I believe these will adequately prove that Lila was justified in killing Mr. Stine."

I know what those pictures show. They show Lila beaten and bloody. They show her cuts and bruises at different stages of the healing process. I didn't know until recently that Cammi and Lila thought to document everything, just in case. I'm glad they did.

Kinney and Banton flip through the photos, their expressions turning grim.

"Miss Winters, we're going to need to know what happened."

Lila hangs her head for a moment. I see a tear fall from her cheek into her lap. She swipes the wetness away and when she lifts her head, the strong woman I know is in charge, not the victim of a violent attack.

"I dated Drake for a while," she begins.

Lila takes the officers through their relationship and the night of the attack. They interrupt occasionally to ask questions or get clarification on some detail. She leaves out the part about the note that was left on her body and the connection to the Knights of Wrath. As far as the police will be concerned, it was a domestic violence assault and nothing more.

"Why didn't you go to the police after the attack? Or the hospital?"

"Tom, you know exactly why," Tillie snaps. "You know what we do as a club. Lila came home to her family. We have both a doctor and a nurse who were able to assess her injuries. And Lila is all too aware of how many times domestic violence isn't stopped simply by reporting it. She was scared and wanted to put it behind her."

"Fair enough," Officer Kinney concedes. "Let's move on to the night that Drake was killed. Lila, can you tell us what happened?"

"Yeah. I went into the city to do some shopping. I was tired of being hovered over at home and of everyone always asking me if I was okay. So, I went alone. I've done the same thing dozens of times, so it was a pretty routine day for me."

"You felt comfortable going into the city alone after being attacked?" Officer Banton asks.

"Of course she did," Tillie answers for her. "She wasn't attacked by a random stranger. She was attacked by her boyfriend, in an apartment she shared with him. It's not unreasonable for her to be comfortable doing something completely unrelated."

"Please, continue Lila."

"Anyway, I was walking downtown from the shopping district to the parking garage where my car was when someone grabbed my arm and dragged me into the alley." Lila shivers as if it's hard to relive her 'memory' of what happened. "It was Drake. He started screaming at me and shoving me. He had a screwdriver in his hand, waving it around like a maniac. I was afraid he was going to kill me."

"About that screwdriver… something doesn't add up for me." Officer Banton looks at me. "The screwdriver had your prints on it. Only yours. Why would Drake have it and why was it his weapon of choice against Lila."

"My tattoo shop was broken into several days prior. I can show you repair receipts if you'd like. Some of my tools from the backroom were taken, and there was some pretty extensive vandalism. At the time, I didn't know who had done it, but now that I know Drake had the screwdriver, it makes sense. Lila and I started hanging out after things went south between her and Drake. He didn't like that."

"So why not a knife or a gun?"

"Because what better way to get back at us than to hurt her and set me up to take the fall? It's not rocket science, Officer." The glare that Officer Banton shoots me tells me that I took that too far, but I don't give a damn.

He returns his attention to Lila. "How did that screwdriver end up down his throat and when did the gun come into play? He suffered several gunshot wounds and so far, those haven't been explained."

"I carry a handgun in my purse. I've got my concealed carry permit, so I wasn't doing anything wrong. I managed to get away from him and retrieve it out of my purse. I pointed it at him to get him to stop but he didn't. So, I pulled the trigger."

"Only once?"

"No. The first one didn't stop him, so I shot him a few more times. I'm a terrible shot apparently because I missed several times and he kept coming. But he was weak. I managed to get the screwdriver away from him. It wasn't easy. I received several cuts to the hands trying to get it." Lila holds up her hands and shows the officers her scars from the glass picture frame. "When he lunged at me again, I swung at him with it. It went in his mouth. That wasn't my intention but it's just how it happened. He fell forward and he must have jammed the screwdriver further down his throat on impact."

It's a wild story. Lila played the part perfectly and somehow, they managed to concoct a story that explained everything. That couldn't have been easy. But the true test comes now. Will they tell her she's full of shit or is the story just crazy enough that they believe it because, as the saying goes, truth is stranger than fiction?

"If you'll excuse us, we're going to go review all the details and discuss it with the prosecutor."

They leave the room but Lila, Tillie, and I remain silent. This was too much work to have it all undone because we talk now. Tillie checks her watch several times, as well as her phone. She appears to be looking at emails but really, she's texting back and forth with the others.

Two hours later, Officer Kinney returns alone. "Miss Winters, you're free to go. If we have any follow-up questions, we'll contact you."

Lila nods and the three of us file out of the room and down the hall. I collect my belongings, which were already waiting for me at the front and we make our way outside to where Isaiah waits in the vehicle for us. I want to hug Lila, tell her how proud I am of her, but we're not done. Not by a long shot.

Now comes the hard part.

31

At an abandoned warehouse on the outskirts of Atlantic City, New Jersey...

"I believe the price that was agreed on was fifty thousand. Do you have any idea who you're fucking with?"

"Why don't you enlighten me?"

"The Knights of Wrath don't jack around. Either you want the goods or not. Keep in mind, if you back out, I make no promises that the sun will rise tomorrow for you."

The three brothers stand there, trying hard not to laugh in the punk's face. He may be an errand boy for the Knights of Wrath MC but they're the Broken Rebel Brotherhood: Atlantic City Chapter. They don't fuck around either.

"Listen, kid," the tallest of the three says as he takes a step forward. "We're not trying to cause trouble. We just want to be sure we're getting what we pay for." He points to the open back of packed white powder at the seller's feet. "That doesn't quite look like the amount of heroin we were promised."

"It's the best heroin you're gonna find on the East Coast. Knights of Wrath only sell the best. And it's exactly the amount you asked for. But if you've got a problem after the conclusion of this sale, you can always request a meeting with my higher-ups. I'm sure they'd be more than willing to do whatever it takes to convince you there isn't a problem."

"Oh yeah?"

"Yeah. Knights of Wrath also have a weapons side to the business so—"

"Hey, kid," one of the other brothers interrupts.

"What?"

"You talk too much."

"Fuck you. I'm just telling you—"

"DEA! Put your hands on your heads and drop to your knees!"

Agents swarm the four men but the only one to follow instructions is the stupid kid that just sold out his own club. One agent steps forward and lowers his weapon.

"I'm Jett. I believe you've got a tape for us?"

"Here ya go. Between that and the information that we've already submitted to the local field office, I'm sure you've got enough to take down the Knights of Wrath. At least in New Jersey."

"Thanks." Jett pockets the tape. "Keep up the good work."

In the middle of the desert in Nevada...

"What about the girls? The deal was for cocaine and girls."

The man wearing the Knights of Wrath cut strokes his beard and glares at the five Broken Rebel Brotherhood: Las Vegas Chapter brothers. There's no patch to indicate this man's position within the KWMC but that doesn't mean anything. The Nevada chapters have been struggling since Screwball's numerous arrests but they're sure that things will start looking up once they secure this sale.

"The girls are safe and sound at my house. But they're gonna cost extra."

"That wasn't the deal."

"The deal changed."

"You can't agree to sell drugs *and* girls and then take our money and not deliver. We won't stand for it."

"That's where you're wrong. I can and I am. In fact, the price just went up by an additional hundred grand." He grabs the duffel bag of cocaine from the brother's hand and yanks it back. "Let's call it an inconvenience fee for pissing me the fuck off."

"Ya know what?"

"What?"

"You talk too much."

"FBI! Put your hands on your heads and drop to your knees!"

Agents spill out of the van that the Brotherhood drove to the meet. As it happened in New Jersey, only one man ends up on his knees while a tape is handed over to an FBI agent.

∽

Seven hours earlier at an undisclosed airstrip in Indiana...

"It's your lucky day, man."

Jackson Stark and Slade Cochran lead Wayne 'Screwball' Stanton from the plane to a waiting vehicle.

"How do you figure?" Screwball demands.

"Because you're a free man," Slade responds.

Screwball lifts his bound wrists. "Does this look 'free' to you?"

"Let me rephrase then. You're no longer the resident of a ten-by-ten cell."

"I don't know what this is all about, but when this is all over, I'll have your jobs."

"Are you threatening an FBI agent?" Jackson looks at Slade. "He's dumber than I thought."

Before Screwball can argue the point, he's tossed in the back of the SUV, with Jackson and Slade on either side of him, and the vehicle lurches forward out of the parking lot.

"Where are you taking me?"

"There are some people who want to see you."

"Who?"

"Hey, Wayne. I'm curious," Slade says. "How does it feel to know that everything you've worked for, everything you've helped build, will be nothing but a distant memory after today?"

"What are you talking about?"

"Well, there are numerous teams, all across the country, gearing up for sting operations on every single known chapter of the Knights of Wrath MC. Before the sun comes up tomorrow, your entire club, nationwide, is going to know you're a traitor and sold them all out to the FBI and DEA."

32

COOPER

"He's inside and from what Jackson and Slade are telling me, he's pissed."

I stare at the side of the building and wait for the calm to wash over me. It'll come. Just like last time.

"What about Donovan and Shawn?" I ask.

Isaiah glances at Lila and Tillie, as if asking permission to keep talking.

"Spit it out," Lila snaps. "It's not like we don't know what's about to happen."

Isaiah sighs. "Noah and Jace already dropped Donovan at the bus station, thanked him for his service, gave him some cash, and told him to get as far away as he can. He knows not to show his face around here again." He pauses and smiles. "As for Shawn, I believe that's Liam with him now." He tilts his head toward the back window.

I look over my shoulder and sure enough, Liam's Jeep is pulling in behind us. When he cuts the engine, he steps out and opens the back door to drag Shawn out and toss him to the ground. Shawn tries to scramble away but his wrists and ankles are bound, and he only serves to look like a damn inchworm.

"Let's do this," I say and get out.

Isaiah, Lila, and Tillie follow suit. I lead the way inside the building, and it takes a minute for my eyes to adjust to the dim lighting. Lila and Tillie are flanking me, while Isaiah and Liam drag Shawn between them.

There are three men in the middle of the large space. I'd recognize the one in the middle anywhere: Screwball. I can only assume the others are the Brotherhood's FBI buddies. When they introduce themselves, my assumption is confirmed.

"What the fuck is going on?" Screwball demands.

He tries to lunge forward but Jackson and Slade hold onto his arms to stop him. I notice he's not in cuffs, as I requested. I want him to think he has a fighting chance. I want to fuck with him. I want him to know that no matter what, he can't beat me.

"You can let him go," I tell the agents and then to Screwball, "I assume you know who I am."

"Of course I do. Your picture is plastered on every KWMC Most Wanted wall in the country."

"Walls that won't exist after today."

"So I've been told. You'll never pull it off though."

Isaiah hands me the burner phone that has been blowing up with texts for hours. I flip it open and turn it around so Screwball can see.

"That's every confirmation we've received today that the club was taken down. Here," I toss the phone at him and he catches it easily. "See for yourself."

The longer he stares at the phone, the more his body tenses and his face reddens. By the time he's done, he's barely concealing his rage.

"Why are you doing this? We were your family."

"Yeah, you *were*. But that stopped being the case when I had to kill my own father because no one stopped him from killing my mother. Remember her?"

"How could I forget the whore who birthed KWMC trash?"

I clench my fists at my sides, refusing to let him taunt me into unleashing my rage on him before I'm ready. I've got a few more things to say before that can happen.

"You can trash talk all you want, Screwball. If it makes you feel better, go for it. Because at the end of the day, it won't matter. You won't matter."

"I will always matter," he seethes.

"Don't you get it? Or are you so stupid that you haven't figured out how this is going to play out yet?"

Screwball laughs maniacally. "You're the one who hasn't figured it out, Cooper. You put on a good show, I'll give you that, but at the end of the day, these two yahoos are still FBI agents." He hitches his thumbs to indicate the two men at his sides. "They're not gonna stand by and allow you to do any real harm. They know as well as I do that there's always a paper trail for a prisoner transport. People will start asking questions eventually."

"He's right, Cooper," Jackson says. "We're not going to stand by and watch this." He turns to Slade. "I think this is our cue to take our new prisoner in." He points to Shawn. "Oh, and we should probably report Wayne Stanton's escape. That's gonna be a lot of paperwork."

Screwball blusters but he's so angry he can't even form a coherent sentence. Shawn, on the other hand, protests and struggles when Jackson and Slade lead him away.

Before they exit with their new prisoner, Slade glances back and says, "Say hello to the family."

And then they're gone. I keep my eyes on Screwball but address the others.

"Why don't you guys head on outside? We're almost done here."

Isaiah, Liam, and Tillie don't ask any questions. They simply turn around and walk away. Lila, on the other hand, steps closer to me.

"Lila, please. I need this."

"I know," she says. She threads her fingers through mine and squeezes. "I'm not going to try and talk you out of it."

"Good. Now you need to go."

She steps away from me and then, as if it's an afterthought, she reaches behind her back and pulls out the screwdriver I gave her to put in her waistband. I continue to keep my focus on Screwball and when he sees what she has, his eyes widen.

There it is. That calm that I was waiting for.

I give a slight nod and wait for Lila to do the last thing I asked of her. She steps away from me and toward Screwball, the screwdriver held out in front of her.

"Here," she says as she hands it to him. "You're gonna need this."

When he picks it up out of her hand, she turns and walks away like she's not leaving me alone to kill a man.

Screwball flips the weapon over in his hand, again and again, as if testing its weight. The grin on his face is exactly what I was hoping to see. He thinks he's winning. He honestly believes that I gave him the thing he's going to kill me with.

"This is going to be fun," he taunts.

"Yeah, it is."

I bend down and retrieve my own screwdriver from my boot, gripping it tight in my fist. I considered a gun but that felt too easy. A knife, too predictable. But to use his weapon of choice against him? A weird form of poetic justice. Add in the fact that Aiden sharpened it, just slightly, to give me an edge and there's no way I wasn't using it.

"There are a few things I need to know," I say.

"I'll answer any questions you have. Hell, it's not like you're gonna walk out of here to blab so what harm can it do?"

I let him think what he wants. No skin off my back.

"Why come after me? It's been years and I wasn't causing the club any trouble."

"Because your betrayal was never going to be forgiven. Or forgotten. I had to take you out to secure my place at the head of the table. You know how it works."

"I do," I concede. "Why go after Lila?"

"I like a good game of cat and mouse. I like to fuck with my targets. You know that. Lila was a means to an end. Maybe if she'd kept her legs closed, she wouldn't have gotten herself into that mess."

My calm snaps and I lunge at him, jabbing the screwdriver toward his chest. He jumps out of the way and laughs.

"I'll give you an A for effort but you're going to have to try harder than that."

We circle each other and I ask my last question. It's not an important one, not to me, but I want to put Lila's mind at ease, so I'll ask it.

"How did you convince Drake and his friends to do your dirty work?"

"Friend," he clarifies. "Drake and Shawn were the only ones that laid a hand on her. The others were just there for show."

"That doesn't answer my question."

"It's not hard to get prospects to do what you want. All they see is the patch and the pussy. It doesn't matter what they have to do to get it."

"I remember."

"Any more questions?"

"Just one." I stop circling and look him in the eye. "How does it feel to know that the only legacy you're going to leave is the destruction of the KWMC?"

Without giving him a chance to answer, I lunge again, and the tip of the screwdriver grazes off of his arm when he dodges out of the way. I spin around in time to block his attack, but he somehow manages to tear through some flesh and muscle in my arm.

"Burns, doesn't it?"

Blood drips from the wound and stains the concrete floor crimson. "Nope."

"When I kill you, who's going to protect those hot little numbers you call sisters?"

I launch myself at him, toppling us both to the ground. My screwdriver flies from my hand and slides across the floor, out of my reach. Adrenaline coursing through me, I pummel his face with my fists. Blood spurts from his nose and the sickening sound of crunching bone fills the space around us.

Screwball tries to defend himself with his free hand, refusing to let go of his weapon. I take out years of rage on a face that no longer belongs to him. All I see is the look of my father after he killed my mother. And then, even that morphs until the only images in my head are my sister's terrified faces as I opened that bathroom door seven years ago and Lila's beaten features as she lay on my front porch.

"You will never hurt anyone again." I land a blow to his ribs. "The Knights of Wrath will curse your name." Another blow but to his kidneys.

I'm so focused on my assault that I miss him lifting his arm. I miss the way he swings as wide as he can to thrust the screwdriver in my direction. Pain seers through my side and stops me mid-punch. I glance down and see the green handle sticking out of me.

Screwball sneers at me, revealing blood coated teeth, before his head drops to the floor with a thud. My chest is heaving, my knuckles are swollen, and still, I'm not done.

With his screwdriver still impaled in me, I roll off of him and crawl to my own weapon. It's hard to maintain my grip because my hands are so slippery, but I manage and make my way back to him.

"Wake up you sick fuck!" I shout.

He tries to lift his head and can't. "Fuck you," he manages to gurgle.

"No." I grip my screwdriver in both hands and lift it above my head. "Fuck you."

Ignoring the intense pain and the way the room is spinning, I bring it down and plunge it into his neck, severing his jugular.

I stare at him, this man who tried to ruin me, and realize that it's finally over. No more living in fear, no more running, no more Knights of Wrath. It's really over.

I struggle to my feet and start to walk toward the exit. I sway and stumble but manage to get there without falling. I try to lift my arm to push open the door and can't, so I turn to let my body fall against it.

I crash through, landing on the gravel on the other side and the world goes black.

33

LILA

"Lila, honey, why don't you sit down?"

I ignore my dad and keep pacing. I can't sit, not yet. I'll sit when I know Cooper is out of surgery.

"Lila, he's going to be fine." Isaiah steps in front of me and puts his hands on my arms.

"You don't know that," I shriek. "He lost so much blood, Isaiah. And what about internal damage? Don't tell me he's going to be fine when you don't know."

"Lila," my dad says from behind me. "Look at me."

I slowly turn around to face him and immediately collapse in his arms, sobs wracking my body.

"Oh, baby girl, it's gonna be okay." My dad strokes my hair. "Cooper's strong and healthy. He'll pull through this." He guides me to a row of chairs along the waiting room wall. "Both Cammi and Carmen have the same blood type, so he'll get a transfusion and they'll stitch him up. You'll see."

"I… I can't lose him."

"I know."

"No, you don't," I wail. "Dad, I love him so much. And I've never even told him. He told me though. Did you know that?

The night before he got arrested, he showed up at my apartment and told me he loved me."

"I heard."

"And then he passed out and then he was arrested. He said he was going to explain things to me, and he never got the chance."

"Lila, he'll get the chance. Trust me. He's going to have the rest of his life to explain things to you."

"What if—" I slam my mouth shut when a doctor comes through the double doors.

"Are you all here for Cooper Long?"

I race to stand in front of him. "Yes. How is he?"

"He's in recovery. You can see him, two at a time, when he wakes up." The surgeon pulls his scrub cap off his head and balls it in his hand. "Right now though, I need to talk to Lila. Is that you?"

"Yes."

"Mr. Long's sisters are asking for you. They're both in a room receiving fluids after the transfusions. They're absolutely fine but they did ask if it would be okay if you went in to sit with them. If you want it, that is."

"Of course. Someone will come get me when Cooper wakes up?"

"I'll make sure the nursing staff knows where to find you."

"Thank you so much."

"You're welcome." He addresses the others. "It's going to be a little while before Cooper's anesthesia wears off. Why don't you all go to the cafeteria and get something to eat? No sense sitting here longer than you have to."

"Lila, honey, text us when he's awake. We'll be here."

"I will, Dad."

"I'll take you to the girls."

I follow the surgeon to the room and see Carmen and

Cammi snuggled in the same bed. Carmen appears to be sleeping but Cammi is wide awake and crying.

"Aw, Cam, what's wrong?"

"Is he okay? Tell me the truth. I can take it."

"The surgeon said everything went fine. I haven't seen him yet though."

"I don't know what I'd do without him, ya know? He's everything to us. I don't think I could do what he did and be a parent when I'm supposed to be a sibling."

"Yes, you could. And you'd do it because that's what family does. But he's going to be fine so let's not even think that way."

"Right. Okay." Cammi lets her head fall back onto the pillow. "I can't believe it's really over. And you're going to be my sister."

"Wait, what?"

"There's nothing stopping you two from being together. It's only a matter of time before you both give in to what the rest of us already know." She yawns and closes her eyes.

"You think?" I ask, afraid to be hopeful.

"Don't you?"

"It's what I want, I know that," I answer honestly. "But we've got a few things to work out first."

"And you'll work them out. Just… don't hold what he did against him. It wasn't the right thing, but he did it for the right reasons."

I hold on to her words as I sit here and watch her sleep. In my head, I know I've already forgiven him, but in my heart, I'm still trying to catch up. He hurt me. More than I ever thought anyone would ever have the power to do. I understand why but it doesn't erase the fact that it happened.

"Miss Winters?"

I turn toward the door and see a friendly looking nurse standing there.

"Yes?"

"He's awake and asking for you."

My heart skips a beat and that's the moment that I will forever think of as the moment that my heart caught up with my head.

~

Cooper

My mouth feels like it's stuffed with cotton balls and my mid-section burns as if someone is holding a red-hot poker to it. I watch the two nurses as they check my vitals and make sure that my IV is still secure so that the pain meds continue to pump through my veins. My head is foggy and all I want to do is sleep. But I can't. Not yet.

"Can you please go get Lila?"

The nurse dealing with my IV pats my hand. "She's on her way. I promise."

"Okay. What about my sister's? Has anyone called them?"

"They're in a room sleeping, Coop."

The machines beep as my pulse jumps. The nurses finish what they're doing and leave the room. Lila remains by the door, uncertainty in her eyes.

"Hi." My voice is thick and I'm not sure if it's emotion or the events of the day, but I don't care.

"Hi." She takes a few steps toward me but stops short of being within reach.

"Cammi and Carmen are okay?" I ask, not sure how to even begin addressing everything else on my mind.

"Yes. They both gave you a transfusion so they're resting. But they're absolutely fine."

My eyes slide closed in relief. It would be so easy to let sleep take over, now that I know that they're okay and I've seen Lila, but I force my eyes back open. I have a lifetime to sleep. Right now, I have amends to make.

"Lila, come here."

She closes the distance between us and picks up my hand. I rub circles with my thumb, savoring the feel of her skin.

"I am so sorry."

"For what?"

That's my Sprite. She's not going to make this easy, no matter how banged up I am. And she shouldn't. She deserves the world and I'll do everything I can to make sure she demands it. From me and everyone else.

"Everything. But mostly for hurting you." I take a deep breath and ignore the pain it causes. "I sent you away. I said things to you that were cruel and entirely untrue."

"I was there. I remember."

"That night, in the field, I made promises to you and I meant them. I still mean them, despite my actions showing otherwise." I tug her toward me with as much strength as I can, and she sits on the edge of the bed. "I'm sorry that I pushed you away. I'm not sorry that I was trying to protect you. I'll always try to protect you because you mean too much to me to do anything less. But I won't ever do it like that again."

"Was I really just a distraction to you?"

"Fuck no," I growl. "You were never just a distraction. Were you distracting? Yes. But that's a different thing altogether. I tried like hell to keep my distance. As far as I was concerned, you were off-limits. Not only are you Cammi's best friend, but you deserve so much more than me." I reach up and cup her cheek. "I'll never be worthy of you, but I'll do my best to be as close as possible."

"Coop, I…"

"What, Sprite?" I urge when her words trail off.

"I won't survive being hurt like that again. So, if you

aren't sure, like a thousand percent sure, that I'm who you want, then tell me now. Because I can't worry that you're going to push me away again or that you're just going to up and change your mind someday."

"I need you to listen to me and listen carefully, okay?"

"Okay."

"I'm all in. No doubts, no fears, no ifs, and, or buts. All the way in. With you. For now. For life. You hear me?"

"All in? Are you sure?"

"I love you, Sprite. With everything in me, I love you. All the fucking way in."

"I love you too, Coop."

"All in?"

"All the fucking way in."

# EPILOGUE

LILA

Four months later...

"Lila, where are you?"

I look at my reflection in the mirror one last time and suck in a few deep breaths. I wanted to do this the night he was voted in as a full member of the Broken Rebel Brotherhood, but he was still recovering from surgery.

"In the bedroom," I call back to Cooper and force a cough to throw him off.

His footsteps echo on the hardwood floor downstairs and I know I've got moments before he hits the steps and races up to give me a kiss. It's the first thing he does every time he comes home and it's not going to matter to him one iota that I'm 'sick'.

I flip the bathroom light off and race to the bed. I've been laying the groundwork all day with pitiful texts about not feeling good and being bummed that my birthday is ruined. I even asked him to stop at the store and get me some orange juice and soup.

Little does he know, I've been rushing around like a madwoman trying to pull this off. It's my birthday but it's Cooper who's in for a surprise. I hear the creak of the top step and I roll over and prop myself up on my elbow.

"Hey, Sprite." The door swings open. "How are you—"

Cooper drops the container of orange juice and it thumps on the carpet. Fortunately, it's a plastic jug and it's not open otherwise I'd be cleaning up a huge mess instead of trying to knock his socks off.

"What's this?" he asks as he looks around the room and takes in all the candles.

"I'm not sick."

"I can see that."

Cooper stalks toward the bed, shedding clothes as he does, and when his knees hit the edge of the mattress, he's gloriously naked. His cock is standing at attention and my eyes are drawn to it. I squirm in my lace panties, already wet for him.

"It looks like you did some shopping," he observes with a wicked grin.

"I did."

My skin tingles as his gaze travels the length of my body. I bought the lacy royal blue lingerie earlier and I was sure he'd see my car in the parking lot at the shop. Fortunately, he was slammed with appointments. And based on his reaction, he didn't see me.

"You did all of this for me but it's your birthday."

"I know." I reach behind me without taking my eyes off of him. "The outfit is for you but this," I pull out the vibrator we bought months ago when Cooper first dragged me into Sandy's Lingerie. "This is my present."

Cooper snatches the vibrator from me and turns it on. We haven't had the chance to use any of the things he bought that day but it's time. Past time.

"Where's the remote?" he asks.

"Right here." I bring it from behind me and hand it to him. "I didn't know what all you'd want to use first, so the other stuff is in the nightstand."

My words are rushed, and I take a deep breath. I'm suddenly nervous as hell. Cooper trails a fingertip down the inside of my thigh, calming me while simultaneously making me want it all, right now.

"Open up for me, Sprite," he demands in a husky voice.

My legs fall open and Cooper climbs on top of me. The vibrator is still on and he touches it to my clit. My hips shoot off the bed.

"Ah, that's it. I'm gonna take you to places you never knew existed."

"Please… ah, Coop," I plead. "Please.

"Please what?" He lifts the vibrator away from me and raises himself up onto his knees to break contact.

"Fuck me."

"You know what you're asking, right? You remember what I told you?"

I nod furiously. "Fuck me, Coop."

Cooper wraps his fingers in my lace panties and rips them away from my body, tossing the fabric to the floor. He reaches into the nightstand and grabs the feather and silk ties that he bought and then binds my hands to the top rail of the headboard.

He traces my ribs with the feather, trailing a path down to my belly button, over my hips, and then in circles around my clit. He leans down and swirls his tongue around the pulse point in my throat.

"I'm gonna fuck you so good," he whispers in my ear.

He tosses the feather to the side and before I can protest, he impales me with his cock, filling me up. I struggle against the binds at my wrists but can't break free. Somehow, that only intensifies the heat in my core.

"Tell me again," he commands.

"Fuck me," I say on a breathy moan.

Cooper slowly thrusts in and out of me, torturing me, teasing me.

"Fuck me, Cooper."

He continues his thrusts but increases his pace. My eyes are closed as I focus on every sensation he's evoking. My hips rock and meet his until he presses the vibrator against my clit again and I'm no longer able to control any of my movements.

He switches between the different vibrations and each one is more stimulating than the last. I throw my head back and squeeze my eyes shut.

"Look at me."

I try, I really do, but the pleasure is so intense that I can't make my body do a damn thing other than enjoy. That is until the vibrations stop and Cooper slows his movements. My eyes fly open.

"That's it. That's what I want to see."

Cooper leans down and presses his lips to mine. He begins to thrust in and out again and it's slow, not fucking, but it's perfect.

"Come for me, Sprite."

Our hips clash and our tongues dance. He grinds his pelvis and hits my clit, sending me shooting off into space. My walls spasm around him, sucking him in deeper, as deep as he can go.

"Ah, Lila," he moans into my mouth. "I'm gonna come."

Cooper's cock throbs in perfect rhythm with my spasms and we ride the wave of bliss as long as we can. Our movements eventually slow and he collapses on top of me. He's careful not to let his weight settle and when he rolls to my side, he tries to take me with him, but the binds hold me in place.

He reaches up to untie me and my arms fall to the bed. Cooper tugs me toward him and holds my head to his chest.

"Happy birthday, Lila."

"Best. Birthday. Ever."

SNEAK PEEK AT BROKEN MIND

BOOK THREE IN THE BROKEN REBEL BROTHERHOOD: NEXT GENERATION SERIES

Ruby...

I was meant for bigger things in this life than being a bartender in small town Indiana. I certainly never thought my military career would be cut short. But the very people who were supposed to train me, help mold me into the soldier I was meant to be, took everything from me. I lost my mind and forgot who I was for a while. I ran as fast and as far as I could, trying to find something, anything, that would make me whole again. I still haven't found it.

Liam...

I know who I am and what I want. My position as the Vice President of the Broken Rebel Brotherhood is the culmination of my entire life and what I was meant for from the moment I was born. It's everything. Or it used to be. A series of repeated one night stands with the new bartender have awakened something in me that I didn't know was there. But she's built walls that I have no idea how to break through.

When a threat emerges and she's forced to reveal her secrets, I realize there's nothing that can stop me from doing whatever it takes to be the one thing she needs: a hero.

PROLOGUE

RUBY

Five years ago...

"No one will believe you, Private."

Sergeant Jensen stands in front of the door, arms crossed over his chest and his uniform as neat as always. I keep my eyes averted as I pull my pants back up, not bothering with my panties. I shove those in my pocket and turn in circles to try and locate my Army-issued uniform shirt.

"Maybe." I shrug. "Maybe not. But I'll do everything I can—"

He shoves away from the door and stalks toward me. I'm not fast enough to stop him from wrapping his fingers around my throat and pushing me against the wall. His elbow grazes my bra-covered nipple and a glint enters his eyes.

"They won't believe you," he snarls. "Because there's nothing to believe." He squeezes, cutting off my air supply. "You got that?"

I open my mouth to respond but nothing comes out so I nod instead.

"You better remember your place, Private. The Army doesn't like it when their Sergeants are falsely accused of sexual misconduct."

Call it what it is you piece of shit. Rape. It's rape.

"Besides, from what I hear, your behavior has been erratic lately. I'd hate for your *mental instability* to become a permanent part of your military record."

The threat is clear: report his actions and I'm labeled a crazy woman who can't hack it in the military.

Jensen releases me and I slide down the wall. He glares down at me and I have to force myself not to shrink away from him. I want to but then he wins. More than he already has.

I tried to report the first time but that went nowhere. Sure, it earned him an interrogation, but in the end, there were no consequences. Except to me. The second time was more brutal and that's when the threats started. For the last two years, I've endured Jensen's attacks and I've kept my mouth shut.

"See you next month."

Like clockwork.

With that warning, he turns on his heel and leaves. He doesn't close the door behind him. He never does. It's like some sort of sick game for him to see if I can get to it and pull it shut before anyone sees me.

I scramble to my feet and do just that. Once I engage the lock, I allow myself to breathe. I suck in air so fast that spots dance in my vision and I sway on my feet. I brace my hand on the wall to steady myself.

I see the camouflage of my uniform shirt peeking from beneath one of the tables and I bend down to pick it up. I stare at the name tag and tears spring to my eyes.

All I've ever wanted is to be in the Army. To follow in my father and uncle's footsteps and serve my country. My mother begged me not to, saying she already spent enough of her life wondering if her husband and brother would survive it, she didn't want to worry about her little girl too.

I didn't listen. The second I turned eighteen, I signed up. It was my dream and my mother's guilt trips weren't going to stop me. Nothing was.

Sergeant Jensen will.

I shove my arms into the shirt and button it up. By the time I'm done, anyone looking at me would have no idea what just happened. My uniform is neat and exactly as it should be. Random uniform inspections are a real thing and failing one is the *last* thing I need.

"Private Banks?"

I whirl toward the door and see the Private who is scheduled to take over for me. He's new to my unit but he seems like a nice guy. Young, hard working, focused. He's all the things I was when I enlisted. He's all the things I wish I still was.

"Hi." I finally find the presence of mind to speak.

"Everything okay?" he asks as he looks through the orders for the day.

"Of course," I say, too quickly. "Why wouldn't it be?"

He shrugs. "You were staring at the wall when I came in. I said your name a few times before you even noticed I was here."

So much for Sergeant Jensen being wrong about my erratic behavior.

"Oh, sorry." I take my jacket off the hook by the door. "Just tired, I guess. I, uh, couldn't fall asleep last night."

"Ah, makes sense. Sometimes I can't sleep. Wanna know a trick?"

"Sure."

"Most people will tell you to count sheep or to drink some warm milk. That never worked for me. When I can't sleep, I always start reciting the alphabet backwards. Usually by the third time, I'm out cold."

"I'll keep that in mind."

I straighten my spine and square my shoulders before pushing open the door.

"Have a good…"

The rest of his words trail off the farther down the corridor I get. I push the events of the day to the back of my mind while I walk to the barracks. My roommate won't be there so I'll have time to shower and wash away the filth that is always there.

After scrubbing myself as clean as humanly possible, I flop down on my mattress and stare at the ceiling. How did I get here? How has my life spun so far out of control that I barely recognize it?

I take a deep breath and close my eyes. It'll be okay, I assure myself. I let the words play on a loop until I almost start to believe them. I can do this. Only two more years and I can get the fuck out of this place.

In the meantime, I'll keep my head down and pray that I get shipped overseas, away from Jensen. Most soldiers like being stationed in the States. Not me. I'd take the middle of nowhere with bullets flying at my head over this any day.

Besides, how much worse can it really get? As I imagine all the ways, my cell phone rings. I roll to my side and pick it up off my nightstand to glance at the screen. It's my mother. I don't really want to talk to her but I've learned that answering her calls is much easier than dealing with the five-hundred texts that follow when I don't.

"Hi, mom."

"Hi, honey."

She sniffles into the phone and I can tell she's been

crying. I sit up and scoot back against the wall, somehow sensing that I'm gonna need something to hold me up.

"Mom? What's wrong?"

"It's Uncle Dusty."

"What about him?"

"He's… he um… oh, honey. He had a heart attack this morning and didn't make it. He's gone."

Numb. A cold and unforgiving numbness settles into my body. I questioned fate and, fickle bitch that she is, called my bluff.

Shit just got worse.

ABOUT THE AUTHOR

Andi Rhodes is an author whose passion is creating romance from chaos in all her books! She writes MC (motorcycle club) romance with a generous helping of suspense and doesn't shy away from the more difficult topics. Her books can be triggering for some so consider yourself warned. Andi also ensures each book ends with the couple getting their HEA! Most importantly, Andi is living her real life HEA with her husband and their boxers.

For access to release info, updates, and exclusive content, be sure to sign up for Andi's newsletter at andirhodes.com.

ALSO BY ANDI RHODES

Broken Rebel Brotherhood

Broken Souls

Broken Innocence

Broken Boundaries

Broken Rebel Brotherhood: Complete Series Box set

Broken Rebel Brotherhood: Next Generation

Broken Hearts

Broken Wings

Broken Mind

Bastards and Badges

Stark Revenge

Slade's Fall

Jett's Guard

Soulless Kings MC

Fender

Joker

Piston

Greaser

Riker

Trainwreck

Squirrel

Gibson

Satan's Legacy MC

Snow's Angel

Toga's Demons

Magic's Torment

Printed in Great Britain
by Amazon